Princess to Save

Book one

The Temptation Within series

By

Roxie McDugger

PLANETTOPIA PUBLISHING

PLANETTOPIA PUBLISHING

Princess to Slave

Copyright ©2014 Roxie McDugger

Cover design and Editing by: Big Bang Book Service

This book is a work of fiction. Any similarities to real people, living or dead, is purely coincidental. All characters and events in this work are figments of the author's imagination.

EBook

ISBN-10:1941246958

ISBN-13:978-1-941246-95-5

Print

ISBN-10:1941246966

ISBN-13:978-1-941246-96-2

Dedication

For my dear husband, PB.

Thank you for always being there for me whether you are near or far. Even though there are many people who gave up on me, you never did. Because of that I am eternally grateful.

Just remember forever + a day 121397

Love, Your Gem

Chapter 1

This is not a "Once Upon a Time" beginning. This story begins with two large men who are both delivering a delicate, rather small, and petite woman to a villa on the outskirts of a Roman city.

One man named Jacos has a thick dark beard covering his face to hide deep dark pits on his face that were caused by a sickness and a rash that had attacked him when he was a child that goes down past his chin. Jacos has a deep accent. He looks mean, but even though he can be strict he does have a kind heart. He only does this job because he wants a better life for his family and takes on spare jobs to provide for them.

The other man, named Nicolai, has wider shoulders and a small head. He looks peculiar, having no beard with his top lip almost being split in half and another scar going up inside his nostril. He has a large gap in his front, upper teeth and is missing his pinky finger. Nicolai is opposite of the other man with a low voice. He can be very mean to the slaves he delivers, at times hitting and kicking them and making them do the majority of the heavy labor. If the person they are delivering is a rather pretty woman, he almost always tries to have his way with them—that is as long as the contract specifically states they arrive "unharmed or hurt". It is very true he does not care for others feelings and just wants the money for each delivery he makes.

The weather is very cold. The wind blows fiercely with the moon reflecting light down upon them.

Finally, the three travelers notice the beacon of lights shining in the far distance toward the city where they are headed. The trip is so vicious that they forget how long they have actually been on this mission. In reality, it has only been a mere three days, but to them it seems like an eternity. The horses let out a loud neigh as a large thunder of snow falls in the distance, crashing atop a tree with a giant thud. The heavy limbs hit the ground, frightening the horses. The icy limbs glimmer against the light of the moon.

The woman they are to deliver tonight is named Helena. She is telling everyone that she used to be a Princess from a very small island south of Sicily. That was before she was kidnapped, sold, and forced into a lifetime of servitude. She is being taken to another man's home by these two men.

The three travelers finally reach their destination and are wet, cold, and very hungry. Jacos bangs heavily on the wooden door. A large man in Roman army attire, with greasy long blonde hair and a scar that looks like a horseshoe across his chin answers the door. Nicolai grabs the heavy iron chains attached to the cuffs that are wrapped around Helena's small wrist, giving a heavy pull on them and yelling, "Come on, Wench! You heard the man." The man lets them enter and escorts the three tired travelers into a darkened room with heavy draperies tossed over the window panes. A tattered and torn couch sits in the corner and a small fire burns and crackles in the distance.

The three people huddle closely together in front of the flames, trying to warm themselves. Nicolai roughly grabs Helena by the copper colored collar that is around her neck, pushing her out of the way "Move out of the way, you bitch!" he yells rudely to her then gives an evil grin as he watches her fall to the floor and scrape her knees and forearms.

Jacos sees this happen and helps Helena up from the cold floor. Returning to his squatted position, he warms his hands and gives the other man a dirty look and says, "What is the matter with you? This is why I hate making deliveries with you! I swear, you are so fucking cruel at times. She, too, deserves some of this warmth! Did you forget that she was the one who helped gather the wood for the fires when we traveled, after you hurt your ankle? Don't forget, she also cooked for all of us to make sure there was food in our bellies! She, at least, deserves to be treated half way decent. She is not a dog. She is a human."

Nicolai takes a large drink of hot cider then looks over to Jacos. "I do not fucking care what she did to help us on the way here. I have not had the best experience traveling here and not had the company of a woman in some time. I told you we should have had our way with her when we had the chance. But you're a fool that has too much pride and dared not to touch her!" he says with liquid dripping from his face.

Jacos jumps up and punches Nicolai in the nose and says, "Fucking idiot. Do you not know how to read?" Pulling a small scroll with light brass around the top and bottom of the parchment out of his pocket, and he continues, "The instructions specifically state, **they said slave with the number: LXXII CXCVII (072197) is to not be harmed or mistreated in any way!**" He rolls the scroll back up and ties the red string around it, sticking it back in his pocket.

The same soldier with the blonde hair that answered the door hears the loud chatter and comes to inspect the noise. He walks just inside the room, saying, "Dominus wants this slave to be moved. Follow me."

Jacos, Nicolai, and Helena begin to walk down a hallway that looks even more dark and dreary. It is even colder in this area than the room they were in prior. The roof where the large beams hold it up are leaking slightly, water splashing about their heads as a small mouse runs down the path, looking for food.

***

As Helena is led into the dim and rather moist hallway, thoroughly tied and bound with shackles around her wrist and legs and rope tied around her upper arms, she feels the jewels of her snug collar around her neck fall against her breast. She wonders how this new Master will be. Will he let the rules and punishments slide? Having been punished numerous times before, she knew what things were acceptable and what things were not, but every man is different. She is unaware that this time she will be pleased with her new owner. In the past, Helena was teased, tortured, and made to believe that she was nothing.

Helena wonders what the look on his face will be. Will she be efficient; will she be pretty enough? The main question lingering in her mind is: will she be able to please this man that she will serve?

She is told to stop and kneel as she hears the squeaking hinges of a large door in the shadows open then close. She begins to tremble, hearing his footsteps get closer. Helena slowly lifts her head, trying to catch a glimpse of her new owner. She can only see a silhouette of this man. He looks to be medium build with broad shoulders. She quickly fixes her eyes on an area of the floor and stares at it, trying her best to not look up.

***

He walks in and smiles softly, noticing the marks across her chest and back. She stares at the floor, shaking nervously as she hears him ask in a very calm tone, "What do we have here? A very beautiful lady, indeed. Release her from her shackles and rope, but leave her collar on."

Jacos begins untying the rope while Nicolai fumbles with the heavy shackles. The man of the house looks over her body from head to toes. He cannot help but see her legs and takes careful note of the fresh cuts and the dark purple bruise that has formed across her knee. "What happened to her knee and to her hands? Why is this? She has calluses and blisters on her hands? I specifically said she was to not be harmed or injured! Or have any injuries come to her," he said sternly.

The two men look at one another and one says nervously, "But, Dominus... the slave, she helped us on the way here. This journey was the roughest we have ever traveled before. She cooked for us, helped build our shelter, and gathered the wood for the fire. Was that wrong?"

The man looks over at the two, shaking his head. "I see no problem with some of that. It shows that she is not afraid of hard labor. But what of this bruise and the deep cuts, scratches about her arms? They look very fresh. She is kneeling awkwardly like she is uncomfortable and in pain."

Nicolai glances over to the large bruise that covers the majority of her knee and the cuts that are on her small arms and says, "She is a clumsy one. This one is... reminding me of a drunken ox trying to carry supplies up a large amount of stairs."

Jacos slightly bows in front of him then yells, "This is not true, Dominus! The words that come from his tongue are lies! My name is Jacos and it is a pleasure to make a delivery to your villa. I have heard great things of you and your house. And this here is my partner, Nicolai. He is the one who shoved her to the floor shortly after our arrival here, causing her to have that bruise and the cuts on top of her arms. She is not clumsy, but will make you proud to be the owner of her. She

15

does know how to cook and it's also true that she did help us build shelter quickly when the harsh winter winds and snow came about without our notice. If you do not mind my saying, in all honesty her knowing how to build shelter the way she did I do find a bit strange. Not many women know how to do this. She says she is a princess, but I do not believe a real princess would know how to do all the things that I witnessed her doing. She may be a bit crazed."

The man nods his head, letting out a loud breath. "I see," he says. "Thank you for your honesty, Jacos. As for you, Nicolai, I will be subtracting ten of the twenty-five Denarii from your pay. You will remember next time you make a delivery to me that when I say no injuries or harm I mean just that! You are the one who caused her injury and bruising so there will be a dock in *your* payment only. Now, I still thank you both for making the hard, strenuous journey in this crazed winter weather. To show my gratitude and noticing the storm is still rather dangerous, you both may eat some soup and bread, and then are welcomed to stay in the guest rooms down the hall and in the morning and may be on your way." The two men look at each in shock to hear this, agree to the arrangements, thanking the man of the house before leaving Helena alone with her new owner.

Still placed on her knees, Helena feels the silks draping down her curvy body and smells the scent of the flowers in her long, thick, brown hair. She notices the smell of pinecones, cinnamon, and berries that is lingering in the air. With her new owner looking down at her, she feels his eyes as if they are burning straight into her soul with him being able to see just how broken she really is.

She hears her new owner say to her in a calming voice, "You may look at me. I will do no harm of you. I promise."

Helena holds onto the sound of his voice. It is like that of a trance that has come over her. She swallows hard then gets the courage to glance up at him, and is shocked by his appearance. This man looks like a God. His hair is dark as onyx, just to his neck, his eyes a grayish blue. His teeth are almost as white as pearls. He has a medium build with large shoulders and muscular arms and chest. He has a marking just across the front part of his chest that goes down his shoulder. It looks like a sun spitting fire from it and what appeared to her to be different shapes of a spear head going across his arm. This man has a scent that makes Helena's mouth water; he smells like a forest just after a rain fall. He has a calming effect in some way. Maybe it is the tone of his voice, the way he presents himself, or possibly it is his scent. She looks around, noticing it is only the two of them in the hallway then tilts her head, smiles softly, and whispers low, " What shall I do now, sir?"

***

The man traces his fingers through Helena's thick, brown hair. He holds her close, with her leash held tightly in his hand. Her trembling hands run up his leg as she begins biting her lip. He groans low, and then she feels the cold leash across her flesh. She leans in and hugs his waist, holding tightly and not wanting to let go. She is hoping this is not a dream. The small tears trickle down her face.

He wipes away her tears, speaking low. "Who do you belong to?" he asks her as he kisses her neck slowly.

"You," she replies. Her breathing is a bit harder. "I belong to you, sir."

He looks at Helena like he has been blind his entire life until now seeing the sun for the first time ever. Then says, "You will never have to worry about being harmed again while under my protection, I hope you know this."

***

Helena thinks back to her last Master. That man was very cruel and treated her horrible, like a wild animal. He would have never addressed her as kindly as this man. She ponders a bit then realizes that maybe this man, whom she now kneels to, will be a better owner. He seemed to be more merciful and let off a calming effect. Is Helena dreaming? She snaps back into reality as she feels his warm hands drift down her cold body.

As he picks her up from the cold floor, he kisses her deeply. Helena smiles brightly, feeling his warmth. She whispers, "Yes, sir, I know this now." She sighs, hoping that she will finally be unharmed and that for once in a very long time it is safe to love and try to trust again, and be loved as well. She sits at his feet and submits to his every need; this is how to repay the man who has opened her mind, body, and soul. She knows deep down that this Master will protect her always.

Helena awakens from a long deserved sleep and looks around the room. The room is large; the walls are a light tan color with blue wavy lines going around the top and cobblestone floors. The room has two giant windows; one window has a balcony that looks across the rivers that are far below. The other window looks out toward the mountains. There are animal heads hanging over the fireplace; to show as trophies of her Master's victories. A large painting hangs on the wall that shows his ancestors. Another painting is hung next to the fireplace that has a sheet over it. She wonders what this painting is, but decides not to look and to respect her owner's wishes of keeping it hidden. Next to the bed, is a cage with birds that are white with pink tips on their feathers. They let out a beautiful, calming tune. In the other corner, sits another cage with a very colorful bird like a rainbow with a bright orange beak and when it sings, its voice is not so calming. It, instead, lets out a loud, annoying noise like that of a chicken being choked to death. Helena chuckles and stares at this odd looking bird. She laughs at the sounds it makes and guesses that this bird is to let her new owner know when something is wrong and to alarm him of that fact.

On the table across the room, fruits and cheese lay on a silver tray. She sees a few things hanging on the door: a whip, a paddle, some rope, and leather ties. She shivers a bit, hoping to not have to go through that pain again. Helena drops her head in her hands and begins to cry low. She sees the red marks on her wrists and ankles from the rope that cut deep into her skin the night before when they brought her in to see her new Master. She traces her hand across her collar; it is not as heavy as the others had been in the past. This one is light with small red jewels that drip off it in layers. She had a few others. One was silver with pink jewels, and another was a rose collar with the stem but no thorns. But this one is her favorite, because it is the most comfortable.

Helena sees her new silks hanging in the distance that were purchased at the local market. They are very stunning and come in many colors: red, white, black, green, and blue. A gorgeous black dress with gold trim is in the middle of the silks, along with ear rings and bracelets. The dress was the most stunning garment she had seen. Before she came here, it was rags or a bag with a rope tied around her waist. She still cannot believe she got so lucky as to be chosen by him. Out of all the slaves, he chose her.

She smiles brightly and looks over on the bed and sees her Master lying there, still sleeping peacefully. His dark complexion glistens in the rays of the sun that are just peeking up from the mountains. His dark hair is barely touching his shoulders.

Helena lies beside him and watches him sleep. She barely touches his large arm, but wishes she could be wrapped in them and feel his breath on her bare skin once again. Helena has never had a Master of this kind before. She can't even recall the last time she slept on an actual bed. She hasn't had the pleasure in a long time. It was normally a pallet on the bare floor, or a cage with some straw with her leash tied tightly to a post. She had no leash this morning when she awoke. It felt quite different, like she was free, but she shall not run away. She trusted this new Master to keep her safe and not hurt her in the way the others had.

She glances down at her lightly tanned body, seeing the small but long scars across her arms, breast, and legs; many more covered her back as well. She remembered when each scar was added, vividly. They were to remind her that she had acted out, and to remind her to never do it again. One was for not kneeling fast enough, another for not responding correctly, wearing the wrong clothing, not asking Master if she could purchase clothing; the list went on and on. She did these things a lot, so she was punished a lot.

She thought to herself how silly it was to receive a lashing for these incidences. Helena was not the best slave, but she did try her best. Helena is hoping to please this Master as best as she could. She gets up to wander her new surroundings. She sees the sun has melted all of the snow from last night's hectic storm. She is happy to see the sun. It was the first time in three days that she had felt the warmth of its rays.

She walks out to the garden to listen to the birds in the dogwood trees. The smell of the fruit and nuts that lingers in the air overpowers the scent of the flowers. So she stops to smell a rose that blooms tall and proud in front of her. Seeing the pool with the small waterfall, she stands beside it to appreciate the sounds it makes. Helena has never seen anything so beautiful.

Wanting to enjoy the beauty a little longer, she sits by the pool and dips her feet into the warm water. She sees her reflection in the water and notices that her green eyes are a little brighter today. She feels her hair cascade down her shoulder as she leans forward. It used to be longer, down past her hips to be exact. Before it was cut off as a punishment. She sighs. She preferred it before and missed her long tresses.

She sits back with her hands around her knees, rocking back and forth and enjoying the landscaping. She scoops up a small handful of water and puts it down her top to rinse off. She puts some more on her face, feeling the makeup that dried and smeared from her many tears that she cried the night before.

As she lay back to allow the sun to dry her, she heard her Master calling. "Girl, where are you?"

Helena frantically rushes toward him, hoping to not be in trouble since she had not woken him. She walks to the entry way and peeks in. She sees him sitting in his chair. He looks pleased as a small smile forms on his face. A gentle breeze crosses through the room, blowing her silks away from her skin; the silks were white as the clouds in the sky and soft as powder on her skin. She has brushed her hair, pinning it up slightly and revealing her face; a few of the lilies that she picked just for him nestled between the strands. She glides across the floor and sits at his feet.

"Good morning, Master. I hope you slept well, and I hope the food is to your standards."

Master grabs hold of her silver collar, pulling her to him and placing her on his lap. He nuzzles his face into her neck, kissing it softly and smelling the light vanilla fragrance coming from her. He responds in a seductive, "Yes, it is all wonderful", as he traces his fingers over her soft skin.

She shivers from his gentle touch, feeling the goose bumps rise over her body. She smiles softly, knowing she has done well to please him. She leans in to receive a very slow but deep and passionate kiss. She traces her hand across his face; her other hand sliding down his arm. She feels the strength in his arms as he holds her tightly to him, the muscles in his arms flexing. Helena feels the man's warm breath against her skin as his hand gropes her breast that has been exposed. Master looks at his new slave with pleasure.

He asks her, "What is your name?"

Helena looks at him and responds in a quiet voice, "Helena is my name, sir."

He replies, "I do not like that name. I will give you a new name that is more Roman when the time is right."

"What is your name, sir?" she questions.

He looks at her, removing her from his lap and placing her on the floor beside him. "For now, you can call me Master. Also, I go into town and trips afar frequently. When I am away from here, you may come and go as you like. The town's people know who I am, so you must remember to not disgrace my name."

Helena is surprised to hear this, but agrees to these conditions. "Yes, Master."

They return inside the large villa where he shows her which rooms she may and may not enter. One room he shows her was his meeting room. It was wall to wall with shelves that had books, maps, and an array of papers crammed into tight places and maps that hang on the walls that showed the stars alignments. This is amazing to Helena and she stands in awe at everything.

She knows her history of her people and ancestors. She recalls stories that her grandfather would tell to her and her siblings of the Romans and the different tribes. She recalls the stories of the Romans setting villages on fire for not helping them fight during war time. The Romans would take the men to be sent to work in the mines, while the women and children would be sent to work as slaves.

***

Master glances up from the papers, noticing the surprised look on Helena's face and gives a warm smile. She reminded him of a child seeing the moon or the ocean for the first time.

Master clears his throat and walks to a large shelf in the far right corner of the room and asks, "Are you able to read? Because if you can, you may read any book you please on this shelf."

Helena glances at the rows and rows of books and smiles, answering. "Yes, I do know how to read. I know how to write, too, Master."

, "Good, thank you for sharing this information. I am glad to know this, but we will keep that between us. Slaves knowing how to read and write are frowned upon in these parts, but I believe I can trust you. I will tell you…that when I am in meetings or in this room, you are to be outside this door and I will attach your leash to the ring. You are not to speak to anyone else unless I am present. Is this understood?" Helena nods. "I wish for you to always look presentable at all times. And I will not be able to escort you every time to market so if you wish to purchase a new dress or silks that, too, is fine, but you will only to be allowed to purchase one a month and you will be allowed to put the cost under my name and send the tally to me here. It is fine they know who I am. Plus, I will have one of my guards go with you."

**

Helena smiles thanking Master for his kindness as she realizes that this man will be different than the one in the past. She finally feels at ease.

Chapter 2

Helena loves to wander; going into town, meeting new and interesting people. She does not trust many, having been mistreated in the past. It has taken a lot to trust this new Master, and she finally feels at ease knowing she will not have to worry about being sold again or traded for something silly.

On this particular day, it is more humid and hotter than normal. Instead of going into town, she swims in the pool and tries to cool off. After her swim, she decides to get a snack and drink a single glass of wine. After drinking the scarlet liquid, enjoying the taste of a finer wine than she had ever had, she sits down on the couch that her Master had just recently bought. She gets comfortable and lays down to rest, feeling the cool breeze roll in the open window from the nearby mountains. Against her better judgment, she drifts off to sleep and dreams about how she became who she is today; especially the man who broke her heart and ruined her trust in others, forever.

She was once a princess in one of the biggest families in the far southern islands. Not many people knew of their land; it was that small. Her father was a somewhat fearsome man, not taking anything from any person, and her mother was even worse. Helena's father was King Dand. He was very

protective of his family, King Dand was a very tall man,
standing close to seven feet tall with broad shoulders and
shoulder length black hair that let off a purplish tint when the
sun would shine down on it. He had thin lips and a slight
jagged chin. He spoke in a deep Scottish-like accent and was
well known across the small islands for torturing people that
disgraced his family by placing them underwater and if they
survived the water torture the person would then be taken to a
small island on the eastern area adjacent theirs where a
volcano had erupted many years prior and killed all the
vegetation, leaving only scorched trees and dried lava, and be
left there to parish. Their Royal Army would make sure no one
would leave the island by planting very sharp daggers in the
sand around the island so anyone who tried to escape would be
stabbed in the bottoms of their feet and develop a horrible
infection within a day.

Her mother was Queen Rhona. She was an average
height woman, standing roughly five feet three inches. She had
fiery red hair with black tips that went just to her hips, and
eyes green as the pastures and high cheekbones with thick
perfectly shaped pinkish lips. Queen Rhona was a very hard
worker, which was odd for being a queen. But, it did not bother
her for others to know this. She knew it would help to learn
different trades for when her husband, the King, and their sons

were off at war. She would still be able to run her kingdom.
She made sure her daughters, Princesses Helena and Lacey,
could fight and fend for themselves. The young ladies were also
taught how to mend their own clothes and how to cook. Queen
Rhona made sure her daughters could be prepared for
anything that may arise. Queen Rhona was not a woman to
upset while her husband was away, because she would take
punishments too far. But it took a person stealing, lying,
cheating, or committing murder to get the worst of all
punishments. Those that would do so would be thrown in the
deepest part of the dungeons and fed very little until they went
insane or begged for death. When the queen felt the time was
right, she would give the orders to execute those by beheading
or being disemboweled. Helena's parents made sure their
people were taken care of. They were strict but also fair,
spending hours listening to the citizens of the city on what they
would need or ideas on how to help the people or lands where
they lived. Citizens would stand outside the corridors for hours
just to be able to see them and able to thank her parents for
keeping them safe from intruders. The Princesses of King Dand
and Queen Rhona was well known for their beauty and
mischievous pranks when they were younger, and their
brothers, Patrick and Neil, were always on the lookout for their
sisters.

*Back then, Helena fell in love with a guy named Justus.
Justus was a slender man who had large hands and coarse, red
hair. Justus was not an attractive man, but he did have a kind
heart and that was all Helena wanted. He treated her very well
and spoiled her as often as he could with the best wine that
money could buy and the prettiest flowers that grew in the
lands. Justus even once gifted her a pony that was black with a
white diamond shape in the middle of its head. She named the
horse Brazen. Justus was a gentleman to this Princess. King
Dand and Queen Rhona could see how happy he made their
daughter and how her face would light up every time someone
mentioned his name. Justus would take trips from time to time
to sell items or retrieve items like the finest silks to the rarest of
jewels. If you were trying to find an item and had problems
finding, then Justus was your man. But Justus also had a secret
he was hiding, and no one knew what this secret was. He was
very keen at hiding it from others and could also fool and
manipulate to get what he wanted.*

*One night after dinner, Justus questioned the King and
Queen about one of his soon to be journeys. He explained to
them that he and Helena would have to take a ship and travel
afar to the main land close to the Orient for some rather
expensive spices. Justus asked the King and Queen if Princess
Helena may travel with him and promised he would take the*

best care of her. Helena's parents put their soul trust of her in Justus' hands.

The King and Queen saw no problems with this and agreed to their daughter joining him on his travel. The following day, Helena journeyed off with Justus. The journey was long and hard; the boat ride was very rough on Helena and made her very ill. All she could smell was fish and the salty sea that rocked the boat back and forth. But eventually they arrived on land. Helena had never been so thrilled to see dry land. The two walked for one day; at night they took shelter near a ravine because the trees were thick and could shade them from the sun, though the weather was humid. Thankfully, Helena remembered her father and brothers teaching her and her sister how to build a fire and make a sleeping area. At day break, the two awoke to eat wild berries and drank a small bottle of water. Then they were on their way again. By midday, they saw the steeples of buildings to a very large city in the North Eastern area in the mountains. The town was bustling with activity, and seemed to have anything a person could want; beautiful buildings, large trees for shade, and exotic animals all created a picturesque area that she loved to be a part of. There was also so much that they could do, including going to plays and eating the local cuisine. It was the most *exciting adventure she had had; she'd never left home before. She didn't think it could get any better.*

But later that first night, after seeing one of the plays, Justus asked her, "You know? I have been thinking about how we are going to get back to your homelands, my love. Your family didn't give you a lot of funds."

"We should have just enough to get back; we just have to be careful," she replied.

Justus nodded in agreement, but he was a very greedy man and did not love her. His secret ended up being that he went from place to place finding ladies, wooing them, and tricking their families into believing that he loved their daughters so he could take them on trips and sell them at auction houses. As Helena slept, Justus executed his plan. He went to the auction house that they had noticed when entering the gates of the city. She was so far away from her family that they would never know she was in trouble. The auctioneers had seen her with Justus when they had come to town and agreed to put her up for auction.

The next morning, three large men came into the room and snatched her up, forcing her into a round cage. They stripped her of her clothing and jewels. She was so scared that she just curled into the fetal position and cried hard. She heard people shouting numbers through her tears, but she tried to tune them out as much as she could. Before she knew it, she was sold to the highest bidder for 45 Aes. Her belongings were sold to Justus, giving him more than enough money to get back to his homelands.

He then proceeded to take her belongings that were precious and close to her heart; including a gold locket she had with a picture of her and her parents in it. It had been a gift from her parents for her 21st birthday, and now it was gone. She was so heartbroken. She told the man named Samo who bought her who her parents were, but it didn't matter. She told them she was a princess daughter of King Dand and Queen Rhona, but the towns people laughed and mocked her. Helena didn't look like a princess. The heavy chains, iron cuffs, and collar caused her to slouch and left scarring in visible places. She was never allowed to have any clothing and was made to wear nothing but bags. Princesses dressed in the finest clothes and jewelry of the time. Her hair was matted all together from the mud—a princess always had perfect hair.

Samo was the first one to abuse her. Saying he was not nice was an understatement; he was a very large man who smelled, didn't smile, cursed at her, beat her, cut off her long chestnut brown hair, and then slapped on a collar with a leash attached and stuck her in a cage underground. It smelled horrid in the cage, and it got very cold at night and very hot during the day. Samo would sometimes bring her out just to tie her to a post and whip her. It would all but rip the skin off of Helena's flesh. The more she would shriek, the more he would beat her.

After a while, she learned to bite her lip and grit her teeth as not to make much noise, so the beatings would not last as long as they did in the past. He would then throw her back underground in her cage. She got used to it after a while. She would sit in her cage, seeing the rays of sun beating down on her, and would pick at the dropped food on the ground. She would pick up a stick or a rock and draw little pictures in the dirt, trying to remember how her life was before that. Her owner would buy more slaves and do the same things to them as he had Helena.

After a few years had passed, he allowed her to come up to his house to live. As long as she obeyed his rules, she would not be put back in the underground cage. One morning, after waking from the pallet with straw that she slept on, she walked around the room that belonged to her owner. Helena walked past a mirror in the corner and noticed her rags that hung on her thin body and her collar that was rusted was very heavy and gave her headaches often. Her hair was very long before, but now it was very short just below her ears and was matted together. She looked like a wild person that had lived with the creatures in the forest. She saw all the scars across her body, along with the dried up mud that was caked on and across her body. This is not how a Princess should look. But, she was no longer a princess. She was a slave.

Even as he slept, Samo held her leash tight in his hand. She wished he would just drop her chain. She didn't know where she would run, but she would run somewhere, anywhere in the lands to be free from this creature. She sighed, knowing she had no chance of escaping. After lying back down on her pallet, she fell asleep to the sound of the ice and snow falling outside. Hopefully she would be able to sleep through the night and not be awoken by her master on top of her. But, like most drunken nights, she was not holding her breath. Maybe she could kill him this time, but then if she failed or the others found out they would kill her.

The next morning, she awoke to see her leash completely on the floor. Helena was still half asleep and thought she was seeing things. She sat up, wiped her eyes, and looked again. Her leash was on the floor. This may be her only chance to get away! She stood up quietly, looking over at the bed where he lay, and saw him curled up with another slave. Helena bent down, picking up her leash and turning around quickly to run as fast as she could out the entrance of the house and threw the gates, into the thicket across the way. Her chain dragging behind and getting it stuck in the limbs. After getting herself untangled, she continued to run and escaped with no incident. She couldn't believe it!

She walked for days. The weather was different than usual. It was raining and it was hot and humid with the sun shining down on her during the day and snow at night. After several days, Helena found a waterfall with a cave and set that as her home. She found sticks and rocks to make weapons.

One of the best things Helena ever did was snap her collar off. It had been on her for so long that when she grasped it, the collar all but crumbled in her hands. Her accommodations weren't the best, but it was better than living with a master. Still, she felt so lost. She was so far from home.

She survived unnoticed for several days, but then one day when she was picking berries, she stepped in a trap and was captured again. The men who found her thought she would be very pretty if she were cleaned up and put in the right clothes. So they took her back to a slave house, cleaned her up, and put her in some decent silks. They knew they would get a very good deal from this one.

Since she had escaped, her hair had grown longer again; past her shoulders. After the men had cleaned her up, she heard them say how they thought that she would stop a man in his tracks and bring in a lot of money. Helena cried after she heard that, because the last thing she wanted was to be sold to another abusive master.

The next day, she walked up on the auction block with shackles around her waist and rope tied tightly around her ankles. Her leash was dragging behind her and her collar was once again snug around her neck; so tight she thought she may choke to death. You could not help but notice the freshly made marks across her small body; the blood trickling down her legs, breast, and back. The auction started again. She heard men and women shouting the highest bids.

In the distance she heard a man shout, "6,000 Denari!" Everyone stopped, turned, and stared at this man. Was this man insane? The man had won the auction, walked up, and paid for girl with special instructions that "She shall not be harmed in any way, shape, or form. She is to be in silks, and not covered in a bag."

The men took her in the auction house, cleaned her up, doctored her wounds, and got her ready for the long journey to her new Master. It took them a few days to get to their destination.

Helena recalled walking into his hallway the very first time. She remembered the scent of cinnamon and pine while entering his home. But the thing she remembered most was the look on his face; his soft smile, his calming voice, and his kiss that made her mouth water as their lips touched for the first time.

Helena awakens on the velvet blue sofa and she smiles softly, knowing she is finally safe.

Chapter 3

One night, Helena is patiently waiting as Master is in a council meeting. She stands at the corridor outside the meeting room, her head lowered as not to make eye contact with others around. The guards that are standing post make rude comments to her, saying, "If sir likes you so much, why hasn't he named you? Even dogs have a name."

Helena never thought about this before. She reaches up and presses her jeweled collar to her chest. She hears a man speaking inside with Master but cannot make out what is being said. It feels like forever that she has been standing. Her feet and back hurt and she is very tired.

Master finally comes out of the meeting room. She notices he looks very tired. Master walks over to her, untying her from the heavy metal ring that is attached to the wall. Little is said as they walk back to the east chambers. Helena wipes her eyes and tries to hide the fact that she has been crying.

Master asks her, "You, what's wrong? Why are you so silent? You act as if Hades will visit soon."

She walks over to the table and pours him a glass of wine, her hands shaking, afraid to answer. She finally replies,

"Master, I have been here for a while now and still I do not know your name or which house I serve. The guards say I am lower than dirt and less important as a dog. Because even dogs have names."

Master begins to go into a fit of rage. He demands to know who has told her this. Helena takes cover behind the ivory table. Master storms out of his chamber to his garden where he asks Minerva (the goddess of Wisdom) to give him a sign of what to do.

Helena wanders the halls looking for Master in fear that he may be out for blood. She hears men talking, thinking it is him. She rounds the corner. "Oh Master, there you are!"

She stops putting the torch down low to see the faces of the two guards. They were the same men who were guarding the meeting room. She feels something bad is about to happen. As she is about to leave, the guards grab her by the back of her head and drag her like a wild animal up and down the hall by her leash. The guards laugh as they spit on her, call her names, and relieve themselves. Helena cries, gags, and holds her breath.

One of the guards spouted out. "Since she doesn't have a name, let's brand her and call her 'SCORTUM'" (which means low-class whore). To brand her quickly, they heat up a tip of a sword until it is bright red. She can feel the heat from it and see the evil look on the guards' faces. Master hears the chatter and noises from afar and rushes to see what the commotion is about. As the guards have her up on her knees holding each arm, her head forced back, the guard presses the scorching metal into her upper arm. The guards laugh and chant, "Scortum, Scortum!" Helena goes into shock from the smell of the burning skin, blood, and pain as her body goes limp and she passes out.

***

Master rushes up on the crowd and is appalled and furious by what he sees. He yells at the top of his voice, "What do you think you are doing? Stop! Let go of her now!" as he pulls out his sword.

Petrified, they drop Helena and bow to him as they all stammer in fear repeating, "Dominus, we are sorry. We did not know she meant this much to you." Master picks up Helena and takes her back to his chambers. He calls on a healer and prays that Hades stays away from her bed. As the healer makes a rooted tea for Helena and cares for her wounds. Master prays for Apollo to heal his slave. And he asks for wisdom from the Goddess, Minerva.

The healer says, "Dominus, she will heal quickly but she will have the scar. If you wish, I can make a salve that she can use to help make the marking not as dark." Master then pays the healer 3 silver coins and thanks her for what she has done. But as the healer is leaving she says, "Dominus, excuse me for saying this, but I have heard the stories of how you once were. But, I can tell that you do care for this slave...You have a kind heart, not many men of your class care as deeply for his servants or slaves. She is lucky to be under your protection and serving in your house."

***

Helena awakens from her rough night, still sore, and feels the burn from her arm. She sees a small bowl with white salve in it. It is white with green leaves. Helena picks it up, putting a bit on her fingertips and rubs it into her wound. It eases the burning sensation and then it feels cool, goose bumps popping up across her arms. The light smell of aloe and green tea leaves surrounds her senses, calming her. Helena sees her Master sitting in his chair. She tries to be quiet as to not disturb him, reaching for her mint tea. The birds chirp outside as the sun begins to rise over the mountains as the rays of sun shined in his face.

***

Master awakens to see Helena sitting up in her bed. She looks better than the night prior. Her color has returned to her face and her eyes look much brighter. He smiles, letting out a big sigh of relief to see she will be fine. He moves to sit on the bed and says, "I prayed that Apollo would heal you and that Hades would stay clear of your bed last night. They both heard my prayers."

"Master, I am so sorry that I disobeyed you. If I had stayed in the bed chambers..."

Master stops her and says, "You questioned me of my name, the house you're in to serve, and why I have not yet named you." I prayed for Minerva to give me the wisdom to tell you and it is time I do this. You serve the House of Felix. My name is Cato - meaning wise. The reason it has taken me such a long time to give you a name is because I wanted it to be fitting for you."

Helena looks deep into his eyes, giving him a warm smile and touching his hand. "I understand, Master."

Cato then says, "I have decided that you will now be called and known as "Calli" in Roman it means "Beauty". You have had a rough night. my Calli. Get some rest and I will tell you more about my house tomorrow when you rise."

Calli is so excited about this that she has a hard time sleeping. As she blows out her torch she says," I can now say my name is Calli, I serve The House of Felix, and My Master is Cato."

■■

Chapter 4

Calli is jarred awake with the sounds of birds and other animals crying out. She hears a thunderous noise that shakes the villa, causing the candles hanging in the room to go sideways and everything on the table beside her to roll off onto the floor. Her small pictures hanging on the wall go crooked. She jumps out of bed, fully awake but scared out of her mind. Another rumbling sound echoes through the villa.

"What in the world is going on?" she yells, quickly dashing out of her room. Rushing down the hall when another small rumble happens making Calli grab hold of the wall, she finally finds Master Cato, who is in his meeting room. "Master Cato, what is that noise and shaking that is happening?" she yells in fear.

Cato looks up from his papers and says, "Calli dear, no worries. It is just the sky talking and the ground answering. All is well and you should not worry. My villa can withstand the shakes of the underworld!"

Calli puts her hands out to her sides to catch her balance and jumps, feeling the ground beneath her feet quake once more. "Master, are you sure all is fine? The ground is talking more than the sky is!"

"Yes, I am sure. If you do not believe me, which I do not know why you would question me on this, but if you like you can go investigate it and see for yourself. Go on, go look."

"OK. Fine, I will do just that. Let's hope the ground does not wish to swallow me," Calli says in a snappy tone as she turns around. Cato watches Calli sway her hips back and forth, walking away. He chuckles then says, "Of course the ground will not swallow you up, silly!" Calli turns to him, sticking her tongue out at him and turning back around to walk out of the villa to the garden to investigate the noise. "Ahhhhh! Ahhhhh, Master Cato! Help me! Please?" Calli cries out.

Hearing her cries of terror, Cato runs as fast as he can to save her, making it to the threshold of the door to see Calli by a tree that has been half up rooted. The pool had an enormous crack, causing the water from the pool to flood half of the garden area surrounding it. Poor Calli is covered from head to toe in mud, slipping and sliding all over the ground. He sees one of his guards trying his best to rescue her, but he, too, was also falling into the mud. To watch this is very comical and Cato can't help but let out a loud belly laugh.

Calli holds onto a tree limb, trying to walk back toward Cato. "Master, help me please!"

"Ok, ok hold on," Cato says still laughing between words while he steps off the concrete. "It's ok, Calli. I will make sure you will not get hurt. Look into my eyes and walk to me slowly and then give me your hand!"

"Ok, Master!" she says a look of fear across her face reaching out for him. Just as he takes hold of Calli's hands Cato loses his grip and slides down the muddy slope, followed by Calli who slides and lands right beside him on her stomach.

Calli lifts her head with bits of mud, the muddy water, and grass all over her. She spits bits of the ground out of her mouth. Cato, sitting on his rear, looks over and asks, "Calli, are you ok?" He busts out laughing, seeing her covered in all the mud, grass, and dirt. He cannot help it.

"Master, what are you laughing at? You should see yourself because you, too, are covered in all of this. I am freezing!" Cato and Calli look at each other again and laugh even harder.

"Ok! Well, I would say this would be a good time to go to the bathhouse."

With the help from a few of the guards, Cato and Calli are finally able to get out of the mud. They both walk in the bathhouse area that is in the back of the villa where Cato and

Calli strip their clothes, letting them fall to the floor. Calli looks around this enormous area. The walls are off white with dark green titles around the top of the ceiling. There are enormous plants in the corners; the smell of jasmine and lilies are strong and it automatically calms those who enter the area. It is very warm and steamy in this area and with the steam being very thick, it is difficult to see. She hears the sounds of the waters rushing in. The sounds are the same as a water fountain.

Cato shows Calli an area where she can bathe in peace with no one to bother her and says, "This is something new. Even I haven't used it yet, but I will allow you to and please let me know if you like it."

"Wow! Thank you so much, Master! This place is just amazing! It looks like a piece of heaven!" she says, glaring up to the sky to see a large square shape that has been cut out of the ceiling. There are two pipes that go inward to heat the water that is inside this wooden bucket overhead. It catches the rain water in the bucket and has very thick cloth fabric with holes punched on top that keep the debris out of the inside. The other fabric that is cut out is the exact size as the bottom of the bucket. IT has a small chain attached to the side that is falling down so the person can simply pull the chain, allowing the inside fabric to move to the side of the bucket where there are small holes pierced   allowing the water sprinkles down below for the person to bathe. Calli is still in shock from the bathhouse and how it looks. She had no idea it would be so beautiful inside; it is truly breath taking. A small song bird flies in, perching itself along the window adjacent to where Calli is looking down at her body.

Calli can see the mud creased into her breast and the small scratches where the twigs caught her. "I still do not understand how people enjoy to be rubbed down in this. I cannot stand the feel of it. Just makes me feel even dirtier." She feels so uncomfortable being covered in now dried, caked-on mud. It will take her forever to wash it off. Calli reaches over, picking up the small rag that is beside the bottle of different oils and a hardened bar of brown wax that has small leaves pressed down into it. Picking up the wax, she rubs it all over the cloth and begins washing all the debris off. The water is so warm from the pipes rushing the hot air into the bucket; it helps loosen her aching muscles that have formed in her neck and shoulders. She traces the wet cloth across her stomach then bends her head to the side, feeling the water run down into her hair. Tossing her head back and opening her mouth, she tastes the water as it runs down her throat and out of her mouth. Picking up a few strands of purple lavender flowers and crushing them into her hands, she rubs some mint smelling oil across the hardened wax once again and throughout her hair. She feels a cold misty breeze blow in, the feel of the cold water against her skin causing her nipples to harden. She arches her back to trace the very soapy cloth down her legs and back up toward her inner thighs. Just the feel of this warm water and the oils and fragrance of the flowers begins to make Calli's heart rise. She reaches up to pull the cord to the opposite side, causing the water to turn off.

■■■

Calli turns around to grab the cloth on the small table and sees Cato standing there. "Master! If I may ask, what are you doing in here? I hope I did not take too long; that was not what I intended to do."

She stands there, seeing his perfectly shaped body. His chiseled chest and the hair on his chest making him look even more attractive. Calli's mouth waters and she lets out a small groan as she looks at him. She feels the small drops of water drip down across her head, the small area still fogged up making her feel like she is in a dream when he begins to slowly walk over to her. She sees the muscles in his arms. They make her feel safe, wishing that they were wrapped tightly around her body. Calli can even see the smallest muscles along his shoulders and pecks twitching with a small breeze that has blown through the tiny area. His unshaven face makes him look like a rugged soldier coming back from a lengthy war. His legs remind her of a work horse pulling a large wagon full of bricks. The half smile with a devious look in his eyes makes her almost faint.

***

Cato smiles and can't help but notice Calli's freshly wet and cleaned body. The way it lets off a light glow against the tiles. Other men enjoy a very thick woman, but Cato thinks that she has the perfect body with curves in the right spots that turn him on. Her waist is not thin, but just a small amount of thickness shows off her stomach. Her breasts are not big but they are not small either. Her lightly pinkish, tanned nipples harden with the feeling of an even stronger breeze blowing in and circling around her. Calli's brown hair is wavy, having small ringlets at the ends. It reminds him of a wave coming in from the shores of a beach. Calli's eyes are a bright green color, like emeralds that shine when placed in the sun. Her mouth has the perfect lines on the sides and it set off her perfectly heart shaped, pink lips. She is, without a doubt, the most beautiful woman Cato has ever seen. He thinks she had to be sent down from the gods just for him.

Cato picks up the cloth, walking over to where she is standing. "I hope I did not startle you, Calli. Here, let me help you," he says in a low, seductive tone.

Cato begins to slowly dry her skin, patting it across her shoulders. His rough hands feel how soft and smooth the oils made her body, running his hands across the middle of her back and paying close attention to soak up the small water drops that are still trickling down her body. Calli lets out a low sigh, holding her hair up off her shoulders as she feels his strong hands trace down her body. She loves the feel of his hands as they trace across her body.

He makes her feel so safe. She cannot fathom the last time any man was so kind to her. She turns around and opens her eyes, seeing Cato still standing there in front of her. "Did I do something wrong, Master?" she asks, waiting for a response.

"Oh no. Nothing at all, my dear." Cato sees her tracing her tongue across her lips slowly then bending down to dry off her legs. He walks up to her, tugging the cloth that is still wrapped tightly around her pulling her into him. He whispers, "I do not think you realize how much I want you and how badly I wish to feel myself inside of you, Calli. I have to have you now!" Before Calli could reply with how much she, too, wants him, he leans over and kisses her. Not hard, but slowly she feels his hand reach up to place it over her jaw to slowly open her mouth. Then his tongue traces across hers and she feels her pulse race and the palms of her hands get sweaty as she wraps her hands behind his head, letting out a small moan of pleasure with her. Exhaling, she pulls him closer to herself. Then with a quick force he pushes her backward and into the corner of a wall.

Cato presses against her harder with both of his hands placed on top of her perky breasts with his fingernails slowly pinching her nipples, each move making Calli want him even more. Calli is so surprised by all of this. She reaches up and pulls the small chain to the water bucket by mistake, sending the remaining amount falling on top of them. She feels the water rushing down on her and she feels her body pressed against the cinderblocks with Cato tracing his tongue down every curvy inch of her body. With her legs on either side of him, she feels her back arch even more as his hard cock enters her wet pussy; the feeling of him rotating his hips and thrusting, making her beg Cato for even more.

***

Her voice echoes through Cato's ear of her a whimpering moan of pleasure. Cato clenches his jaw when

Calli plunges her teeth in his shoulder and her nails cut deep in his back. The water from the bucket is still dripping on top of them, but he doesn't care. Her hair is a wild mess so he pulls her hair back in a fistful, wrapped tightly around his finger. He grabs hold of her, walking over to the small bench then placing his legs on each side of it with Calli on top of him.

"I want you to ride my cock, fast and hard. Do you understand?"

She feels her face turn red with a blush. "Well, I have never done this but I will do my best to please you, Master." Tracing her hand down his chest, she bucks herself forward feeling him go deeper inside of her. "Oh my," she exclaims, moving her hips back and forth in a small circle.

Sitting up barely on the tips of her toes and placing her hands against his chest, she rears herself up and then moves back down on top of him. She places her feet on either side of his head, leaning back to feel his throbbing cock enter her as she arches her back and pushes her wet pussy down around him and then moves her hips back and forth faster with each thrust she makes. Cato lifts his head back, grabbing Calli by her tiny waist and slamming himself deep inside of her, hearing her let out a loud moan. The feeling of pure ecstasy rushing through her body is like the feeling of her floating on top of a cloud. She reaches up and runs her hand throughout her hair, and bites down hard on her lip and tosses her head back, feeling him dig his nails into her waist and moving her back and forth as fast as he can, making loud grunting noises with each hard push he makes inside of her, feeling her muscles contract and expand each time. From out of the blue, Cato stops, picking her up off the top of him and spinning her around to place her stomach down on the bench. He leans down, slowly tracing his tongue down the spine of her back. Calli lets out a low moan from this feeling.

Cato notices the oil in the corner. Picking it up, he squirts some on his hands and rubs it quickly between his hands to warm it up then passionately rubs it across Calli's shoulders and neck down, and the center of her back.

She lets out a groan. "Oh Master, that feels wonderful!" She was surprised to have this done to her.

He whispers in her ear, "Well, if you like that then you will love this."

Cato places his hands on each side of her hips, placing her bare round ass against his hardened cock and rubbing it across her wet throbbing clit before placing the head just inside of her and grabbing a handful of her hair until her head is bent back. He thrusts deep inside her and she lifts up her ass just enough to grind hard into him, feeling him almost loose it with each pounding thrust he makes. She very slowly slides off of him and then with the same speed glides himself back in her wetness. Calli feels the pleasures of all of him pushing herself up with her arms, wrapping her legs tightly around his waist and pushing him deeper inside of her. Calli lifts her head up, letting out a moan that echoed through the entire bathhouse, her body shaking moments later. Cato grips her hair as hard as he can while thrusting into her and thinking she may go through the wooden boards. She hears Cato moan and shout cuss words as he releases his cum deep inside of her. They both lay across the wooden bench, panting.

Calli was in shock at what just happened. She never imagined it like that. She enjoyed every part of what just occurred. It was even more satisfying than she thought it could be. She rolls onto her stomach crawling off the wooden bench and onto the floor.

Cato looks at her. "What are you doing? Are you ok?"

She smiles. "Yes, of course I am, Master. I thought what we just did was wonderful!"

Cato smiles, seeing the cloth next to her on the floor. He picked it up, kissing her on top of her head. "I agree."

He covers her with the long cloth then goes to the bath area. Calli sits up wrapped in the cloth, still mesmerized by how passionate he is then stands up and follows Cato to the bath area. That room is the largest of them all, making the one she was in seem like a hole. The colors in this room are tan and brown with white zigzags across the tiles and floors. She sees ivy wrap itself around the walls; large elephant ear plants on the floors in large vases surround the corners. A small vase of flowers sits on the table. It has poufy orange petals with the stigma being a dark blackish, silver color. They let out a strong scent that makes Calli sneeze and her eyes water. She sits down with her knees up under her chin, watching Cato lay back to wet his hair. He looks like a god, the water running down his body. She is now completely comfortable with him.

Cato notices her staring out of the window, dreaming. He asks her, "What are you thinking about? I know there is something you're curious about. Was it what we just did? I hope I was not too rough with you. At times, I do not know my own strength."

Calli's face blushes with a bit of embarrassment. She has never been asked her opinion on this topic. The man who once owned her would rape her repeatedly. She gazes at Cato through all the steam that has gathered around the bath area. "Master, I enjoyed everything that we just did. I believe my head is still spinning and my body is trying to come down from the heavens. I did have one question. I recall you telling me a while back that you would tell me about your house and your family; do you mind telling me that story, Master?"

Cato takes a deep breath then plunges down into the water, jumping back up from the water and shaking his head back and forth. He smiles. "Yes, of course I will. But, I must say that I have never had anyone be so interested in me before."

Calli chuckles and replies, "Well, since I came here I would love to learn more about your family and your people. If that is ok, Master."

Cato walks up the steps. "I do not mind telling you of this. I am hoping that you will enjoy this story." He pushes himself with his strong arms on top of the edge, sitting down beside Calli and beginning to tell her the story of his life and his family.

Chapter 5

Growing up, Cato's family was a big part of the Republic. His father sat on the Senate and was highly respected throughout the city. He was Cato's hero. No one was better than him. Cato's mother was the typical house wife. She took care of her family and did have slaves that helped with some of the chores and the cleaning. His mother still made sure that she was the one teaching his sister, Sarah, how to cook and how to run the household. When his sister finally made the age of 17 she was set to be married to a high ranking officer named Eric. He served under Alexander the Great. He had traveled many places, making friends everywhere he went. He was a good match for Sarah and did treat her well.

Cato was married to a beautiful lady named Moriah. This marriage was arranged shortly after Cato's twenty-sixth birthday. His wife was breathtaking; she was tanned skin, dark brown hair with eyes that shined like the stars and blue like the sky.

Cato's father was poisoned shortly after Cato's wedding. Cato's mother was so depressed and scared by the idea of surviving now that her husband was gone. She wound *up dying of a broken heart. This then left everything in his father's will to Cato.*

Cato was part of the Roman Army and served during one of the many wars, making his way up in rank quickly. His soldiers and those under had the upmost respect for him. He was a strong leader and a caring man. Those people never knew but each night after a battle he would go to his tent and weep in silence, making sure to say a small prayer. He would make sure to walk through the camp asking his other men if they were ok, and then walking up to those that perished that day in battle and placing coins on top of their eyes so they may pay for their ride in the afterlife. He would then go to his tent and weep for the men that he lost.

After the wars finally ended, Cato was able to return home to realize that his wife, Moriah, had died of child birth as well as the child. He was so hurt that he plunged himself into working as a blacksmith part time and also helping his friend, Anton.

He worked very hard and kept himself busy those next five years. He became wealthy by not taking on slaves or servants until five years after. Cato was then thirty-one years old when he lost his entire family. To clear his head, he would travel a long distance. At times, he would travel from the edge close to Africa of Ancient Rome to the other that was so close it was next to the Orient. Cato would also visit his friends and take extra note as how they treated their servants if they did not listen. They, at times, would be beaten. This made him sad and he would turn his back, trying to ignore the issue.

Cato only had a handful of friends that he could trust. Fuscus was Cato's closest friend. They grew up together and knew each other since they were small children. Fuscus' father was the local blacksmith in the city and he was well liked by Cato's father. Cato and Fuscus also rode the horses of the Roman Army when they would drop them off for Fuscus father to tend to. They would help Fuscus' father by grooming and feeding the horses that came in to be taken care of. When Fuscus' father passed away quickly of a heart attack, Fuscus was then given ownership of his father's business.

Fuscus was a very smart young man and had been shoeing horses since he was seven years old. There were many of the people in town who thought with him being not even thirty years old that the business would be ruined. But he showed them by picking up where his father left off, and even more contracts from the surrounding cities. Fuscus was a of average height, had tanned skin, was a very muscular build with scars on his arms, one being a deep scar that was just *underneath his eye that he received the first time he ever tried shoeing a horse. He had dark, black hair with gray streaks throughout and dark eyes. His other friend was Anton. He had worked his way up in rank and met Cato while they were in the Roman army together. Both men got along great after they each had a fight with the other soldiers over the food that was served to them. The soldiers they had the altercation with for some reason thought since Anton was thin he was an easy target to bully. Cato was the one who stood up against them and helped Anton fight them off. After the huge fight, those who were picking on Anton thought differently.*

Anton would help teach the gladiators to fight in the arena and he would also go to the market with the wealthy men and help them decide on which slaves to purchase. People seemed to trust him to help with an important task like that. It was possibly because of the honest look he had about him. Anton was bald with a very thin build and long legs. Large dark eyes bulged out of his head, making him seem homely. He limped when he walked. His wife was Lila. She was very dark skinned with hazel eyes, and a pointy nose and chin. She was a rather thick woman with a gorgeous face, but her figure was not the best with her large hips, large, saggy breasts. She was a woman who loved to spend her husband's money and show

off her jewels and new dresses. She loved to gossip and would
talk about how many slaves they owned.

Cato's friend, Lucius was very wealthy having
inherited everything after his father passed away from old age.
He and Cato would play together when their fathers would go
to meetings. Lucius was a very stern man who was well known
throughout Rome. He was not very tall, barely standing at five
feet five inches, with brown curly hair. Lucius was also known
throughout for his parties and the abundance of slaves that he
acquired. His wife was Camilla and was known for treachery
and her beauty; having long blond hair, silky white skin, green
eyes, and medium firm round breasts. Lucius and his wife were
very rich. They owned all the gladiators in the city. Camilla
was taller than her husband, making them an odd pair, but they
loved each other. Even though she did love her husband, when
her husband was away to market or a trip she would call on
certain gladiators to come service her. She had to keep this a
secret. She would have been the talk of the upper class and
then would have been known as a whore and a disgrace to her
husband. Camilla was sure that she was not the only one to lay
with a slave. Also, she did not want to risk Lucius losing money
over her rendezvous. They would visit Lucius and Camilla
frequently at least twice a week. If Anton had to go away on
business, he would allow his wife to stay with Lucius and

Camilla. Lucius did not mind Lila staying for a spell. It gave Camilla someone to spend time with. The two women would go to the market, drink wine, and go see the Gladiators at the ludus. It thrilled Lila to watch the men practice. Lila knew Anton would help others and give his advice on which slaves one should purchase. The large men would go to one of the ludus', the older men would go to the mine, while the women and children would go to one of the many houses as indentured slaves.

Once, Anton convinced Cato that he needed to buy a handful of slaves to make him money in the long run, and they would be taught at their friend, Lucius' ludus. Cato agreed, paying Lucius for his slaves to be trained, fed, and clothed. Cato noticed he never had any female slaves until one day he came across one slave girl at auction who had a kind look but was also very saddened. Anton informed Cato about schools that trained slaves like her that she can go to that would make sure she would be well taught to submit to his every want and need. Cato did not accept this proposal.

The slave girl's name was Jadeah. She was a tall woman who was rather skinny and her hair was dark red and frizzed out at the ends. Jadeah was auctioned off to pay for her late husband's debts, having to leave her son under the care of her brother. Cato purchased her for one hundred Denarii.

Jadeah knew how to cook, clean, and though she was rather hard-headed Cato could tell that she was trying to learn. Cato tried very hard to teach her. He was a very patient man who tried very hard not to scream. He remembered his father and mother screaming at their slaves and it saddened him when he saw them cringe and hide in fear.

Cato also watched as his friends would beat and talk down to their slaves, making them feel useless. He thought how horrible it was to have to serve under a person who was so cruel and mean.

But he learned a few things as he had traveled. He created the five rules that he thought a Master could follow, making both he and his slave content and happy.

1. *A man who never makes demands, will be a Master who treasures anything you give.*

2. *A man who is calm, will be a Master who will be able to weather your storms.*

3. *A man who has walked the path of peace, will be a Master that can guide you along the path.*

*4.	A man who never stops learning, will be a Master who never stops growing and teaching.*

*5.	A man who doesn't run after you, will be a Master you will never need to run away from.*

He had these painted in red on heavy scrolls and hung them on the wall. But Jadeah was a very hard-headed woman with a quick temper. She did not fear many, and she did not want to be in servitude. She was furious that she had to serve others because her husband owed so many people when he died.

Cato told her, "If I have to give you more than one warning, there will be punishments. I do not like doing this, but you will learn my rules. I have read on your papers you were with two other Masters. Let's hope I will be the last." Jadeah chuckled. Cato glanced at her and said, "Hold your tongue! If I cannot get you to listen and serve under my thumb, then perhaps I can send you to a house where they teach slaves. They are very harsh, mean, and those in charge do not care how much you cry, beg, or plead with them. They will whip you until you submit; be happy I am not like this."

***

Jadeah looked at Cato and realized he was serious. He grabbed her chain and walked her to a back room. She stood in awe as she stared at this enormous room that is dark as night. On one side of the room, the windows were covered with very heavy curtains. High ceilings, a fireplace, a large object that was the shape of an X and had ropes connected to it on each side, shackles on the wall, a bamboo mat with small pebbles that go across the center in a cross pattern all made up the ambiance of the room. There were lit candles across the walls. Adjacent, were hooks that are attached to the walls that hold different size ropes. Pictures hang on the other wall. You could not help but notice the rules that were hung up neatly on the wall and attached to the adjoining wall were a few items he used for punishments, such as a long leather tie that is fringed at the ends, a bamboo stick he had received from his sister's husband as a gift from one of his trips to the Orient, and a metal spread bar he had purchased on a trip.

Jadeah collected her thoughts and asked him, "What is all this?"

***

"Oh, these are things I have collected over my travels, and gifts from friends and loved ones. I never thought I would have to use them to be honest, but you have proved me wrong," Cato replied.

Jadeah looked at Cato with a saddened face and said, "Apologies, Dominus."

"I have been very patient with you, more than I should I have, but if you do not learn my rules I will have no other choice but to sell you." Jadeah was shocked to hear this and began to cry as Cato said, "Crying will get you nowhere, and it will not change my mind." Jadeah dried her eyes and agreed to be taught by him.

The next day, Cato and Jadeah were in the darkened room when he gave her an order. "Kneel at my feet," he said. Jadeah did as she was told, but when Cato's back was turned she spoke rudely to him under her breath. She did not notice he was standing behind her as she was still going on. 'THWACK'!! Her eyes filled with tears as she all but jumped out of her skin. She felt the fringed leather ties go across her bare ass. Cato walked up to her, saying in a very calm tone, "Jadeah, what did you say? I did not hear you."

Jadeah turned to him and shouted. "What!?"

Cato was furious and growled under his breath as he shouted, "Damn it, Jadeah! Have you been to the slave school? Let me tell you how it is; it is a very vigorous school with a female teacher and a male teacher. They are very strict, stricter than I. In case you didn't know… Your training began the moment your eyes opened this morning!" Jadeah stared at the ground as he continued. "I can promise you. I will never hit you across the face or back. You will not like me at times, but you have to be able to trust me."

"For some odd reason, I do trust you," Jadeah said, walking over to the mat and dropping to her knees, with her back straight and hands on her thighs. But after not even five minutes, she was wiggling and shifting her weight from one leg to the other. Cato noticed her movements and walked over to pick up a small whip and snap it to the floor. The sound was that of a bolt of thunder, echoing throughout the room and startling Jadeah.

"Come over here next to the wall and bring that mat," Cato ordered, pointing to the wall that had the hooks. Doing as she was commanded, Jadeah knelt, sitting straight up with her legs close together. Jadeah started to perspire as she felt Cato wrap a small piece of rope around her hair to tie it off her shoulders and then tying the rope into one of the hooks. He took a soft piece of cloth and put it around her shoulders, pulling it tightly and tying it off to two hooks. Two more pieces of rope are tied over her upper legs as her legs are spread wide, tying them together and screwed into the bottom of the wall. Cato walked over to where his items were hanging on the *wall as he heard Jadeah swallowing hard. He picked up his other whip that was very light and wrapped tightly in horse hide, bundles of horse hair tied to the ends; it was a gift from Anton.*

Cato stepped back, rearing his hand back over his head and snapping his wrist as the whip swirled around his head with a loud snapping sound as it barely touched Jadeah's inner thigh. He whipped his hand around again, and her eyes widened as she let out a small shriek. "Are you comfortable?" he asked, stopping to notice how perfectly she was kneeling.

Jadeah glanced up and said, "No, not really Master."

"Good, I'll be back," he said, then walked out of the room.

Jadeah felt her legs cramp and feet and ankles begin to slightly swell up. Her whole body started to feel like needles were going through each inch. She felt her hands sweat and body perspire. She felt tears trickle down her cheeks. Cato took his time. He enjoyed standing in the sun, soaking up the warm rays and eating a small piece of fruit while having a glass of wine. He then took a small walk around his garden, stopping to have a quick conversation with one of his guards. He looked up to the sun thinking that it was finally time to check on her. It had been an hour and he found her in the same position.

Her body was trembling from her muscles aching. Cato had a feeling that she had finally started to learn his rules. Cato then untied her and said, "You can stand, Jadeah." She was so tired from sitting, he then said, "Come, let me doctor your wound." As he took a cream and rubbed it across her large whelp over her ass and upper legs. He said, "This cream will burn, but it will help ease the pain and the whelp will almost be gone by tomorrow."

As the days passed, Jadeah got better at serving Cato. She would travel to the ludus with him. Anton was shocked when he saw her at a feast. He asked Cato, "Is that the crazed slave that you purchased at the last auction?"

Cato smiled and said, "Yes, this is her. Her name is Jadeah. It was a long time for me to train her, but she finally understands my ways and rules."

This specific night the men were playing dice and one of the guest is very cocky, making the statement, "If I roll double sixes, I will wager my sword that my father gifted to me! Cato, what will you place on the betting board for your roll?"

Cato glanced up and said, "I do not have much to wager, my friend."

His friend looked at him and said, "How about that slave girl, Jadeah? Every man has their eye on her tonight. She *is very submissive! I will tell you what I will do for you. I will pay you double the coin of whatever you paid for her at auction and I will give you a boar as well."*

Cato had had a lot to drink that night and said, "The Gods have blessed me with a great slave, and with many blessings. I accept your offer, but I also get your sword and a boar if I win."

The man agreed, picking up the dice as he shook it vigorously in his hand and tossed it to the floor. Two sixes fall in place and the men cheer and laugh as they pick up their glasses of wine. Cato was stunned as he picked up the dice and rolled them around in his hand. He smiled, looking around at his friends who had gathered to see the outcome. Cato lifted his hands to the air and threw them to the ground as one dice fell on a six and the other twirled on its edge. People cheered and laughed, spilling their drinks. Cato began to block out everything that was going on as it was all happening to him in slow motion, watching as the dice showed—a five!

The crowd groaned in total shock as they looked over at Cato to hear him screaming out loud in disbelief of what had just happened.

The men all stood in shock except the winner, who was dancing around and cheering as he smiled and said, "Ah ha! Cato, dear friend, looks like the Gods have favored me to be her owner now. I will give you your coin now, and since I feel bad for you I will be delivering a boar in the morning." The man chuckled, walking away to gloat and brag to everyone who would listen.

Cato walked into another room is very upset and mad at his stupid decision. Cato summoned his slave, who, upon entering, noticed his sadness. She began to kneel at his feet. "Master, you summoned me?"

"No, no need to kneel at my feet. I have done a very stupid thing, and the Gods have punished me on my fucking greedy decision. I have lost a bet in a game."

Jadeah looked at him and said, "Apologies; I am sorry to hear you lost your wager, Master. What did you lose, if I may ask?"

Cato looked up to her, feeling it hard to swallow "I did not have much to wager, so I bet your servitude."

Jadeah's eyes widened and her mouth dropped as she said, "You bet me? How could you do such a thing?"

Cato felt a large lump form inside his throat and his eyes began to tear up. "I am so sorry for this! You have no idea how this makes me feel."

***

Jadeah looked at him in disbelief, her blood beginning to boil. She felt the hot tears roll down her face as she dropped to his feet and hugged his legs

"No, Master, no! Please tell me the words that leave your lips are not true! Please, tell me it is not so!"

***

Cato grabbed Jadeah standing her back up he said, "I am so sorry to say that, yes, it is true. You are now to serve my friend. Please, I do not blame you to be mad at me. I was greedy and bet you."

His friend walked in, rubbing the winning in Cato's face. He threw the bag of Denarii and a gold coin in Cato's hand as he said in a cocky tone, "175 Denarii and one piece of gold – I honestly can't believe you gave this amount of coin for her but she better be worth it." The man grabbed Jadeah by the arm, walking her to the door.

Cato stood in the entryway as he watched his friend saddle his horse and Jadeah walked beside him as they departed. Cato swore after that he would never make a mistake like that again. His friends did not understand why he was so saddened to see her go. Cato was hoping to see her again, even if for a brief moment.

***

Cato went on many journeys. One such journey included visiting his sister, Sarah, and her husband, Eric. Sarah was a petite woman, standing just to her brothers chin, and looked like her brother with the same bluish gray eyes, tanned skin, and dark hair that was just to her shoulders.

Eric was a very large man who towered over his wife. He had very large, broad shoulders with a chiseled chest. His dark hazel eyes and large muscular legs made him seem mysterious, but the truth was that he was a pretty open person. Eric enjoyed horseback riding and practicing with his sword and dreamt of the day he could go to a battle once more, though this time he hoped to not lose a finger like the previous fight. He wanted to keep his family safe so he would practice with his sword daily, jabbing at trees and enjoying the hunt. While Sarah enjoyed the outdoors, it was the smaller things in life that made her happy. She was always laughing at things, and the smile that graced her face while she did was infectious; making the men laugh right along with her, even if the topic was not funny.

One day, Cato had received a letter that his sister had given birth to her second child. Her first child had died shortly after the birth. Cato had just come from visiting his friends, Anton and Lila, who were celebrating with their friends, Lucius and Camilla. Lucius and Camilla were also expecting a child. Apparently, everyone was having babies or expecting them. It made Cato happy for his friends, but deep down his heart ached for his wife and child. He wondered what his son would have looked like; would he have his eyes? Or would the child have his mother's kindness? Possibly, the child would have been courageous like Cato's father.

There was a time after his wife and son passed that Cato fell into a dark and lonely time; he would often visit whorehouses on the outside of town. There were always new prostitutes. He would pay the madam a very high price and would also get his pick of the lady. Cato was a respected man in the city and did not want word to get out of a secret he had been hiding. He did not want the women to know his face so he would wear a mask that would hide his identity. The guard would then escort the prostitute inside the villa and command them to remove her clothes and to leave them on the floor inside. After she would enter the room, she would see Cato inside awaiting her arrival. He would then command her to walk over to the wall and he would walk up behind her and cuff her wrists to the long chains that were hanging from the ceiling and hoist her until she was standing on her tiptoes.

One night, he recalled the prostitute the guard had escorted in. She was very nervous as she was still new to the life style. She knew there were some really twisted, sick fuckers out there. She had serviced them before and a few tried to kill her, so she was wary about another encounter. She should not be too worried about this. Some men wanted a three-some with the man and his wife. Others would just sit and watch as her and the wife would service one another. Or the wife would watch. But that was nay the case in this incidence.

Cato walked into the shadows of the room and watched as the woman stood just inside the door. The lady was like the others before her.

***

She heard a long whistle that would make your skin crawl and then heard Cato bark, "Go to the window and stand facing the wall!"

She did as she was told and Cato walked up behind her to snap the cuffs in place, then walked over and pulled the rope so she could stand on her tip toes. He did the same creepy, uncomfortable whistle. She shivered and swallowed loudly when she heard the sound of heavy boots clacking against the stoned floor as they got louder and closer. She was a pretty woman, standing 5'4" with black, wavy hair that had a plum color tint and hung down to the middle of her back and fell into *ringlets around her face. Her eyes were green and sparkled like the stars; her lips a perfect heart shape and light pink color.*

***

Cato walked up to her, whistling the same tune. Quickly, Cato swung her around to him as he kissed her hard and pressed her into the wall. She tried to trace her hands through his hair, but she could only get her fingertips to touch. She was then surprised when, without warning, he was lifting her up and wrapping her legs around his hips and placing his large hand over her throat as he began to slowly squeeze. She looked into his eyes with fear as she began to whimper, but then it was changed to low moans as she felt his cock begin to press against her wetness. Cato quickly removed his hand from her throat as he saw the terror in her eyes. He stomped away to the corner of the room where he grabbed the ladle of water.

"Sir, are you ok?" she asked, afraid she had done something wrong.

As Cato ran his fingers through his hair, he glanced up and saw her silhouette from the flames of the fireplace as he answered, "Yes, I am fine. Just stand up."

The temperature of the room was stifling. Cato walked to the lady with the large ladle of water that was filled to the top, taking another drink and then grabbing her by the back of her hair and bringing her head back as far as it could go while ordering in a very stern tone for her to open her mouth. He slowly poured the cool, refreshing water into her mouth. He then walked back, refilling the cup and then pouring it over her head. Cato said in a hypnotizing voice, "Stand up and do not move. I do hope you are ready."

***

She turned her head as she heard his voice. Her legs were so weak from standing that they were beginning to buckle. Without warning, she heard a swooshing sound then a loud slap, and then the stinging feeling across her ass. The lady jumped as the pain shot through her body.

***

Cato shouted, "I said, stand up!" She quickly stood and wrapped her hands around the chains, pulling herself to her feet. She had no idea that Cato was very precise and an exact hit with his whips.

He heard a low moan leave the woman's mouth, followed with the words of pleading. "More."

Cato was even more surprised and shocked as he heard himself reply with, "Okay."

He tears some very soft fabric, tying it around the ends of the whip and dunking it in the bucket of water. He quickly snaps his wrist above his head as he sees it land across her firm ass. Standing with her legs wide apart and feeling as if he was watching in slow motion; the fabric that is wrapped around the ends slowly connecting with her. He heard a louder moan echo through the room. Cato dropped his whip, stomping over to her and unfastening the cuffs and watching her drop to her knees as she traced her hand across her bare breast; the other hand down and across her wetness. Cato reached down, grabbing her breast and pulling hard then rolling her very hardened nipples between his fingers.

He leaned in, whispering, "I never said you could touch yourself, did I?"

She looked in his direction, shaking her head and whispering, "No, sir, you did not."

Cato slid in behind her, grabbing a handful of her dark hair and hearing her groan when he dragged his wooden paddle down the center of her back and grabbed her hair with his fist reaching back to deliver a hard blow to her ass. The lady jumped, shrieking loudly and almost jumping out of her skin. Her eyes filled up with tears then her body shivered from the feeling of Cato's teeth gliding down her body.

He pushed down on her shoulders and yanked her head back to cover her mouth with his hand as he whispered, "I figured since I paid for you—I believe I can do anything I want to you. Now, arch your back."

She arched her back, rubbing her wetness into Cato's throbbing, erect cock. He felt her perspired body lean into his, and the lady reached back and ran her hands through his thick hair. Cato's hands reached for her rather large, perky breast while roughly kissing her neck. They each heard one another moan.

"Sir, please!" Cato grabbed her hair, forcing her face and front of her body atop of the stone floor and her back to arch, with her ass sticking up at the correct height so as for Cato to quickly ram his cock deep inside her ass. The lady lets out a painful yell, quickly clawing at the floor and trying to get away. Cato grabbed her hair tightly, gripping her hair while his other hand digs into her lower back. Cato grabbed her by the waist, pulling her back to him and grinding deeper and harder inside her, her deafening screams making him orgasm with the lady falling over to the floor and panting heavily.

Cato stood up, swatting her ass with the back of his hand then walking over and dunking his cup into the bucket. He tossed a bronze coin at her and a piece of fruit. He picked up his moistened clothes and walked to the door, but he stopped and turned to her. "The guard will take you back to your place," he said, then walked out left her alone in the room.

The lady stood, drying her eyes and wiping herself off. She grabbed a few pieces of fruit, looking at her reflection in the silver platter in the process. She spun her hair up with a few hair pins then opened the door where the guard awaited to take her back.

***

Cato did these actions for six more months. Anton and Fuscus have not seen their friend for a very long time, hearing the rumors that Cato was not himself and completely gone crazed. The two friends, along with a few of Anton's slaves, decided to stop by for a visit, unannounced. When Cato walked into the room, Anton and Fuscus could tell just by his outlook that he had changed from a very nice, clean, and respectable looking man to a callus, nasty looking person. He used to make sure that he was very clean and professional looking with his hair being combed a certain way and a clean shaven face. What they saw was just the opposite. His hair was all matted together and dirty, his skin that used to be tanned was now very pale making him look sick. He even had dark circles under his eyes and a strange stench emanating from his body, meaning he had not bathed in some time. He looked and smelled like he had been tossed in a dungeon and forgotten, and to make it worse he was drinking more than he normally was. The two men could not help but see empty vases that used to be filled with wine scattered around the main room.

Anton and Fuscus finally asked, "Cato, what has happened for you to be doing this to yourself?"

Cato plopped down on a chair and said, "What does it matter? It is my life!"

Fuscus questioned, "Where is Jadeah?"

"She is gone!" Cato answered.

Fuscus and Anton looked at each other. "What do you mean? Where has she gone?" they asked.

"I lost Jadeah to a fucking game of dice! I am a horrible person and do not deserve to live! I honestly think the gods are only keeping me alive just to see how much they can see me torture myself before I go to the afterlife!" Cato yells out.

Fuscus and Anton had a very surprised look on their face and Anton said, "Oh my goodness, Cato! Why didn't you tell us of this sooner? Dear friend, we will help you!"

Cato looks at them with a raised eyebrow. "I do not even know where to begin! I do not need help; I will be fine. I have lost my wife, my son, and my slave. I deserve to be alone! Okay, I am just staying to myself."

Anton looked up, calling his slaves that he had brought with him. "I need both of you to bathe Sir Cato, making sure he has his beard gone and afterward make him a decent meal then clean this villa immediately." Cato picked up his wine, finishing it off then throwing it across the room as he shouts, "There will be more auctions coming up in two months and we will not take no for an answer!"

Cato burst into laughter and said, "Next month, my sister and her family come to visit. She is celebrating her son's birthday!"

Fuscus, not paying any attention, blurts out, "Apologies, Cato; I understand that you are still saddened by your wife and son, but you must bathe—you smell and your place looks and smells like that of death and I am waiting to see rats run through here."

Cato shook his head with a snide look across his face, walking out to the balcony and looking out to the waters below. He heard the wind blow through the trees and the waters rushing quickly. Cato dropped to his knees, weeping low and having the feeling of being at his lowest point in his life.

Anton turned to his friend and said, "You fool! Think about it—when your wife was found murdered, it tore your whole world apart! You mourned for four years. Everyone mourns differently so leave it alone Fuscus...we will get him cleaned up and back in the swing of things and he will be ok. Hopefully, he will find someone."

Cato walked to the other balcony, looking out across the garden. He saw the blossoms of the flowers that are just blooming and the honey suckle that was draped over the wall, the wonderful scent permeating the air. The scent of everything combined brought back memories of his wife. He had an epiphany and realized that his wife would want him to move on and find someone to take her place.

Cato walked back in and said, "I believe it is time I do move on. But I must see my sister and her family before I go to any auctions."

The two slaves followed Cato to his bathing area, assisting him by shaving his face and neck region, cutting his long, shaggy looking hair, and also giving him a nice massage with the oils they had found stuffed away. They even washed his dingy, smelly clothes. All of this had taken so long that when they were finished, it was very late at night.

So, the next day while Anton, Cato, and Fuscus were at the market, the two slaves cleaned the villa and made it look almost spotless. Then they went to the garden for the fruits and vegetables that were ready.

Before Cato knew it, two weeks flew by and his sister and her family had arrived. His sister stepped out of the wagon. Her child was named Thaseus and he had curly brown hair just like his father, Eric. Thaseus toddled to the stairs, falling on his rear and looking up in amazement of his uncle's villa. Sarah hugged her brother tightly. He smiled back and welcomed them to his home. After all was settled, it was time to celebrate. The villa was packed with close friends and a few remaining family members. The food was a small fruit tray with honey and a sweetened bread with cherries baked in. Fresh fish, boar, and carrots were served for dinner.

As usual, all of the guests that attended brought a slave to help hand out the food and wash the guests. Everyone was having a wonderful time. Before everyone departed, Eric stood to make a speech, his voice echoing through the area as the chattering came to a halt. "I want to thank everyone for coming, and my wife's brother, Cato, for throwing this wonderful celebration for our son, Thaseus. The gods have blessed my son to have many people to love him."

Eric then reached in a cloth sack and pulled a large, awkwardly shaped item that was wrapped in a dark blue, silk fabric with different shapes and writing with a yellow belt around it. He handed it to Cato, whose face lit up as he began to unwrap the very large gift.

The present was a large shield that Eric had brought back from one of his trips to the Orient. The fabric that it was wrapped in was called a robe. Thaseus wrapped his tiny but chubby fingers around the edge of the shield as someone in the back raised their glass and making a toast in Cato's honor.

***

After the guests left and his sister and her family were in bed, Cato walked in his room where he kept his collections and hung the shield above his fireplace. He then headed outside where Anton, Fuscus, and Lucius were. "It looks like you are doing better and back to your old self, Cato!" Anton said.

Cato smiled and said, "Yes; things are going quite well, but I am surprised that you three have not left?"

Cato could not help but notice a flyer that Fuscus was holding that was speaking of an auction: LARGE SHIPMENT OF SLAVES FROM AROUND THE WORLD...*The Toughest men and Most Attractive women.* It was to take place in 4 *days. Anton, Fuscus, and Lucius were very excited for this event. Cato, on the other hand, was not as excited. But he decided to tag along just in case.*

***

Lucius was the most excited. Depending on the numbers and ages, it could mean more gladiators for his ludus. Fuscus had a contract with the Roman Army. He was the one who shoed the horses and he was hoping to purchase one slave to help him with the contracts since it would be even busier than usual. The gladiator games were only a few months away and everyone from the nearest cities would be there. Anton was excited as well, but he was only going to help his friends choose. Cato thought hard about if he even wanted to attend this and was not sure if he even wanted to have another slave. He had not purchased another since he lost Jadeah; that was at least nine months ago. It would take them at least three days to get to the city. They were hoping the weather would cooperate and it would not be too harsh on them.

The men woke early the next day and only stopped to rest a while, eat, and to feed and water their horses. They finally arrived at the gates of the city. Fuscus, Anton, and Lucius walked around the vendors to check out all the items that were for sale. Just as they thought, it was the normal; fruit of different colors, rugs, jewels (which were probably fake), carved statues, ivory carved animals, and much more.

The men walked up just as they were starting the auction. They were in the very front and watched as the auctioneer began the bidding with the men. There were twelve men. Some are being sold into slavery to repay debts; others were deserters' of the Roman Army or people who refused to help fight beside the Romans. Those that did refuse to help fight beside the Roman Army would watch as the Romans would torch their villages and if there were any survivors they would be killed, or be put into servitude.

Fuscus noticed a young man about twenty years of age. He was a very large man with a large muscular built and blond hair. His calves looked like tree trunks and his hands were enormous, too. This person was rather simple minded, but would be of great help so Fuscus purchased him for less than one hundred Denari.

Now, there were eleven men left to buy. Anton got in for a closer look at them. He paid close attention to their arms, legs, chest, and back. This would be an amazing purchase of gladiators for his friend's ludus! Anton had a very serious look on his face, shaking his head as he walked over to Lucius, whispering something in his friend's ear.

The auctioneer shouted back prices and then Lucius shouted, loud and clear, "5,000 Denarii for the lot of them!"

Cato glanced around, noticing the women. The women were not as pretty as the flyer had stated and Cato felt like whoever made the flyer had lied. The women were to be auctioned off after they were finished with the men. Lucius was smiling from ear to ear as he told his friends and gloated to the others of his wonderful deal. The other men were very upset, tearing up their papers and cursing amongst themselves before walking away.

Anton looked over at Cato and said, "Lots of bitches to choose from. Would you like me to assist you in a decision?"

"If I buy one, should I send her to the school? I do not think I could handle trying to break in another slave."

Anton chuckled. "Cato, your name may mean "WISE", but when it comes to some things, you are not. Maybe I should choose one for you? You are very stubborn at times. I could find you one that you would not have to spend forever training, but I'd choose the prettiest one, and I honestly do not see a pretty one amongst them. These all look rather used, like an old bag that a horse would eat out of. Shit, I would not let my worst enemy fuck them!"

Lucius overheard the conversation between Anton and Cato and decides to give his opinion. "Cato, this is how I look

91

at it: as long as the tits, cunt, and ass are not deformed, diseased, or infected ...it should not matter."

Anton and Lucius laughed as they heard a vendor and a customer arguing behind them.

"Ok. It is up to you, friend. Do you still wish for me to help you decide?" Anton asked.

Cato looked down the long line of female slaves and said, "No; I believe I will decline this shipment. Maybe next time there will be better looking women. There are only seven women being auctioned off and none of them jumps out and catches my eye. I am going to head back home."

Anton and Lucius walked over to the auction house to pay, leaving Fuscus to walk around the auction area and vendors. He heard the auctioneer arguing with two men who were filling out forms. The auctioneer was getting louder, arguing with the men. Fuscus was curious and, yes, nosy, so he got closer.

He then heard the auctioneer say, "You cannot put her in the auction! Like I said before, you will have to wait for next week!"

These two men were trying their best to change the auctioneer's mind. When one of the men said, "This girl we found will bring in a lot of coin! We promise, and we will split it with you!"

The auctioneer threw his hands in the air and yelled, "Fine! Fuck it. The bitch can go last!"

Fuscus is stunned by what he just heard and only saw a quick glimpse of the lady's face. He could tell that she was, indeed, gorgeous. Her eyes sparkled like they had been kissed by the rays of the sun, with a breathtaking figure and looks that envied a goddess. She could be Venus' sister! Fuscus looked around, not seeing his friends anywhere to be found in the area. So he sprinted as quickly as he could toward the city gates, hoping to catch Cato. Fuscus finally caught up, yelling his name. "No! Cato, wait!"

Cato turned around to see his friend bent over, panting and gasping for air and barely able to get out the words.

"You have to come back to the auction area! Very pretty woman—you will want to see!" Fuscus sputtered out.

Cato growled low and then said, "Fuscus! Damn it, I said I already saw the female slaves and found none of them attractive or any I would like to purchase. Right now, I just want to go back to my home."

Fuscus raised his voice to his friend. "But, Cato, there is one slave that is being auctioned off last who is a late arrival! Just go look at her."

Cato was upset and tired, but agreed, and he and Fuscus walked back into the city. Fuscus made his way back to pay the auctioneer for his new worker and to retrieve his horse.

Cato looked up to the sky. "I do not have a clue on what I am to do or why I am still here; just give me a sign!" Cato stepped out from the shade and noticed a perfect rainbow that had appeared just above the auction house. He thought that this must be the sign he was waiting for as he rushed back inside. Cato saw them bringing an elderly woman off the auction block.

There were men and a few women screaming and arguing amongst themselves. Cato looked around for this "very pretty woman" and was just about to turn and leave when the auctioneer yelled out to the crowd, "Due to a late entry, there will be one more auction!" Cato could not believe his eyes when out walked this very attractive, young, rather petite woman. She had dark brown hair and dark green eyes that could melt your soul, and curves in just the right places.

The woman stepped up on the auction block, and Cato looked around noticing everyone so quiet. This woman looked so lost, broken, and afraid, but there had to be a fire hidden under all that. Something about her made Cato's heart skip a beat and send chills through his body.

Everything about her pulls him in! Thank the Gods above! Let's hope she can understand and not be fearful of him. Can this one beautiful woman show Cato moving on with your life is alright? She looked around, seeing everyone yell. Her eyes filled with tears as people started screaming louder and pointing at her. The auction was now packed, shoulder to shoulder from the quick stories of this one beautiful woman!

Cato could not allow anyone to get this slave. He had to have her! Leaping forward and knocking into people, he opened his mouth and yelled as loud as he could from the back.

"6000 Denarii!"

Everyone stopped and gasped, turning to him. One man burst into laughter and then shouted back, "Damn it, Man! Are you insane?"

Cato glanced at the man. "No, I am not! But I do know I must have her!"

"Sold to the sir in the back, for 6,000 Denarii!" the auctioneer yelled.

The people at the auction cursed under their breath and tore up their tickets before Cato knew it. The crowd began to dwindle down quickly, everyone going their separate ways. Cato could hear many of them complain as they stared at him like he was insane for purchasing one slave for such a morbid price. Cato walked up to the auctioneer, paying his very large amount.

He noticed the scared, timid soul being sent back to the auction house to be cleaned up to make her way to his home as the auctioneer said, "Dominus Cato, you got a top pick today. That little slave will be a great investment! Let's hope she can cook for you and whatever else you may wish her to do."

Cato looked up as he smiled at the man and replied, "Yes, we shall see, but she just looks different than the other slaves I have seen in the past. Something spoke to me, telling me to purchase her."

The auctioneer chuckled. "It may be this horrid heat that is beating down upon us that is making you think this, but I will say I have never heard of any person purchasing one slave for that amount that you just paid, but I am so glad you did. Are there any special instructions for her?"

Cato leaned in to the auctioneer. "Yes, there is. She is not to be harmed, scarred, injured in any way; and I wish for her to be bathed and in the best silks that the auction house has. If that last part is extra, I will pay it."

The auctioneer looked at Cato. "It's no problem at all! No worries. We will make sure that she is in the best ones the house madam has. I will tell you that we have a few people who *are good at making deliveries and I will send them, if that is ok with you."*

Cato glanced back, seeing his newly purchased slave being escorted to the house. "Yes, this is fine. But, please make sure that no harm comes to her. She looks very frightened."

"Of course. We will make sure your slave is taken extra care of, Sir Cato," the auctioneer replies.

Cato glanced in the doorway as he saw the lady he just purchased being stripped of her clothes and water being poured over her body. The lady shivered as the frigid water went down her skin. She tried to cover her naked body to hide the scars all across her. Another lady grabbed her hair, pinning it up. They took some purple flowers, crushing them into an old cup and then massaging it into her hair with another handful of small pomegranate berries. The ladies began to question her, "What is your name? And why are you so quiet? You should know that you are going to a very well-known house! Be warned, though, his heart has turned dark after losing his precious wife and child. We shall see how long you last."

***

The woman looked around frantically. "My name is Helena and I was a princess before I was kidnapped." The two

ladies looked at one another, laughing and mocking her.
"Well, guess what, your highness? Sorry to tell you this, but
you are no longer a princess. You are now property of the man
who just purchased you. Be happy you are going to him and
not the whore house!" one of the ladies snapped at Helena.

***

Cato is startled as the lightning crashes outside the window of his meeting room. He hears Calli outside his entry way and then catches a light scent of pomegranate. Cato opens his door to a guard handing him a rolled up scroll with an invitation. It is for the Gladiator Games from his friend, Anton. He informs Calli to ready herself for the next few days. They will be traveling to the city of Pisa.

Chapter 6

Calli is so excited for this journey. She has heard of the games, but has never seen them in person. She heard from others at the auction house where Master Cato purchased her say how exciting and somewhat grotesque they could get. She thought to herself, if she could handle her mother and father's gruesome tortures of traitors, she could handle the games.

Calli looks out the window and hears the rain as it splashes on the clay roof. It is a cold, gloomy day and Master Cato is in the meeting chambers. She was informed the night prior of an invitation that he received for the neighboring city, Pisa. She remembered Master Cato telling her that it is normal for royals to go to the games. Everyone went to the games. Even the peasants. The games are a perfect time for prostitutes to make extra money. The games lasted for hours.

Calli picks out the dress that Master Cato would love to see her in, sliding it over her body as she traces her hand down her arms. She feels the scar that was given to her by the horrible guards shortly after arriving to Master Cato's. Calli thinks to herself, *if they are married, I would hate to see how they treat their wives.*

Calli walks out to the garden and picks fruit from the tree, hearing a small sparrow singing a wonderful tune. The waterfall from the pool in the distance is so relaxing and calms her. Calli reaches down to pick a few lilies and place them throughout her strands of hair. She smiles brightly as the sun's rays that peak out from a cloud like they are flirting with the humans. She stands still briefly and soaks up the rays, looking out across the grassy area and notices the mountains where the snow was just beginning to melt away and hears thunder rumble a distance away. She hopes the rain will stop soon and not ruin their entire trip.

***

Cato walks out on to the balcony, seeing the rain begin to fall again and notices Calli in her dress; motioning her to follow him. It is a rather long destination and it would not be so bad had it not rained the majority of the trip. It is so humid that Cato already feels his skin stick to his clothes and sweat bubbles up on his forehead, running down the side of his face. He just may melt before leaving the villa!

***

Calli feels every piece of clothing she is wearing stick to her. She thought she was going to dread the journey, but is just very thankful that she did not have to walk. Instead, Master allowed her to ride behind him on his horse. She was smart and did think to bring a few pieces of fruit and some wine.

They reach their destination just as the rain stops. Entering the city, they see children playing and running. The vendors are very busy. Everyone is trying to sell something. Cato and Calli enter a vendor and see people selling clay figurines and lamps. The gladiators walk the streets as an announcer screams out their names and skills. They grow closer to the arena. The smell is almost unbearable. It smelled of vomit, piss, and other grotesque bodily fluids that would make your stomach curl. Calli has never been to the games before and it did intrigue her curiosity. Cato looks over to her, leaning in and giving her a small grin as he says, "Just so you know, you do look stunning today."

Calli feels her cheeks blush and smiles as she knows she has pleased her Master.

They walk past the ludus where they hear the Gladiators practicing before they are hoarded out for the big show. The gladiators live and train together. Cato and Calli go to Anton's villa. Calli is nervous; she has heard that the man of the house is nice but the lady of the house was very mean to their slaves. She looks at Master Cato and gives a slight smile.

101

Calli is speechless as they are let in by one of the guards, named Brutus, who is a very large, hairy man with dark facial hair in spots. You cannot help but notice that one of his eyes is slightly sunken inward. He has a greasy face with dark pits over his skin. He looks like he just came from feeding a swine. Calli looks around in awe as she notices the marble decorations, paintings, and flowers, and the abundance of slaves all running around trying to make the villa look perfect for the celebration after the games.

***

Anton enters and hugs Cato. Anton cannot not help but notice Calli and her lavishing dress. Calli says nothing and looks quietly at the floor. "The Gods have stopped the rains, so let us get to the arena before it begins again. Maybe someone will visit Hades in the end!"

The arena is packed and still has a stench of death and feces lingers. Calli watches in horror as two men slash, hit, and stab at each other. In the end, the gladiator looks at Anton, waiting for his answer of thumbs up for his opponent to live to fight another day or thumbs down for his opponent to have a sudden death.

***

Calli kneels at Master Cato's feet, trying to shield her eyes of the outcome. This was nothing like she was used to seeing in her home lands. Seeing a man beheaded or disemboweled was bad! She could not understand hearing the crowd of people cheering loudly for two men who are fighting until one could possibly die. Calli looks down to the ground below then looks over to the area where Anton is seated across the amphitheater. He is very excited, drunk, or both. His wife, Lila, sits next to him, laughing hysterically. Seeing Calli and the scared look she has across her face, Lila gives the slave a calloused look and leans over to whisper something in Anton's ear. They both look at Calli and cackle loudly. It feels like forever for Anton to make his decision, but finally he stands up, patting his head with his sleeve and looking around as he soaks in the sounds around him. Anton gives a thumb up, and Calli looks up at Master Cato, giving him a smile of relief.

The night after the games, the rich celebrate with a big feast. There is wine, bread, fruit, and meat with sauce. Calli understands the customs and the job she is to do and washes her Master's fingers and hands, handing him a glass of wine and then placing food on his plate. Later that night, after everyone had left, Cato and Calli head to the guest chambers when they overhear Lila screaming at Anton. "I don't care how long you have known him and that he saved your life! As long as they are guests in my house, his little slave will sleep in the quarters with the other slaves! Besides, it is just until Cato awakens. If they do not like this, then they can sleep on the streets! What is the worst that could happen?"

***

Cato looks to Calli, noticing the nervousness across her face and shakes his head. "It looks like you will have to sleep in the slave quarters. Anton is my oldest friend. We are guests in his house and I do not wish to disrespect the lady of the house. I promise, as soon as I awaken I will send for you."

***

Calli understands and follows the guard to the cold, dark, dampened quarters. These are more horrible than the arena was. But, Calli reminds herself that she has lived in worse places before. There are planks of wood scattered on the floor with torn woven bags and wet hay. The only warmth was from two torches on the walls, and the water to drink was a trough made for horses and other farm animals while the food was molded.

Well, it is just until morning. She dozes off to sleep. Just as the sun was beginning to rise, she hears the door rattle and the jingling of keys. She thinks it is a guard coming to retrieve her. As the door opens, Calli notices it is one of the guards. She remembered Miss Lila calling him Brutus. Calli asks, "Have you come to bring me back to my Master?"

Brutus glances around and sees the other slaves still sound asleep before he answers. "Yes; come with me, you." They walk down a winding hall and then into another corridor and into a room. It looks like a cell that a Gladiator would be placed in before a match. Calli stands quietly and is then picked up and thrown into the holding cell. Brutus then leaves her there, laughing as he walks away.

Calli yells as loud as she can. She cannot believe what has just happened! That nasty son of a bitch threw her in this cell! Now what was going to happen to her?

***

"Cato, I was hoping you would be going to the bathhouse at 2:00 for the local gossip? The cost is 1 Aes."

Cato agrees and he, Anton, and two slaves go to the bathhouse. Brutus returns to Calli's cell and informs her that after Cato is killed she will then be the property of Anton and Lila along with all of Cato's property. As planned by Lila. A servant by the name of Felicia, who was Lila's favorite, walks by. Felicia became their property because her Master, who was wealthy, did not register. Every five years, each male Roman citizen had to register for part of the Census. Wealthy men had to register and declare his family, wife, children, slaves, and riches. If not, he would be sold into slavery and his riches confiscated. This is what happened to her first Master. Felicia was once a female gladiator. Felicia was a very good gladiator, but since very few women fought as gladiators and the Romans did not approve of women participating in the arena they were not often seen. She was then sent to work in the quarters of Anton and Lila. Felicia was to make sure that the male fighters kept their strength up so she would cook for them. She mostly made food from barley and fruit and would deliver it to them. That day, Felicia was delivering food to the gladiators when she heard Calli calling for help.

Felicia looks at Calli with a weird face. "What is your name, and who is your Master?"

"My name is Calli, and My Master is Master Cato!" Calli yells. "Oh please, you must help me! Miss Lila and Brutus are going to kill my Master!"

Felicia looks at Calli like she is crazy and says, "Oh please! Why would My Domina and a guard kill your Master? What would they accomplish by doing such a thing?"

Calli shakes the bars attached to the cell door. "Brutus says that they will receive all of my Master's property, including me! I beg of you, please help me!"

**

Felicia looks around, noticing no guards in sight and then puts her tray of food down on the floor, rolling her eyes. "I must be insane for helping you and I may be whipped until my skin is hanging off of my body for betraying my Domina, but you better hope you are right! Sit down on that bench and be quiet. I will be right back!" Felicia sneaks around the corner and notices a sleeping guard with the set of keys around his belt loop. Reaching down slowly, she unlatches the keys from the guard's belt and quickly rushes back to the cell Calli is in. She finally finds the correct key and unlocks the heavy door as quietly as possible, and then Calli squeezes through.

"Oh, I can't thank you enough!" Calli says.

Felicia replies in a whisper, "My name is Felicia, and you're welcome. I will help you find your Master, but that is all I will do! You must follow closely to me. I know this area like the back of my hand, but we must hurry!" Calli and Felicia rush out of the holding area and pass the villa to the bathhouse. They find the back area of the bathhouse unguarded. The two slaves rush in and frantically begin to look for Cato, hoping they are not too late!

***

Cato and Anton are in the back of the bathhouse, catching up on the local gossip. There are two slaves guarding their items. The slaves are the ones who are plotting on how to get rid of Cato. Lila has promised freedom to the two slaves if they do this for her.

Anton, Cato, and a few other men of the city are having a water fight when Anton cannot help but notice a prostitute walking back and forth, eyeing him. He looks over to Cato and says, "Have fun, my friend. I have other things to go do." With the other men also leaving to go to other areas of the bathhouse, Cato is left alone.

Cato wets his face with a soft cloth, rubbing bath oils and other lathering agents until it is covering his entire facial region. He leans down his face closely to the water, trying to rinse the soap off, when out of the blue one of the slaves jumps behind Cato and grabs him by the neck and pushes his face completely under the water. Cato fights back with all his might, grabbing the slave's hands and twisting them as far as they can go until he hears a cracking sound. The slave screams in pain as Cato pushes himself away from the attacker and gasps for air. Trying to realize what just happened, he looks around the room frantically. The other slave had followed a different man into another area of the bathhouse, who had left the area for a short time to get clean sheets. He thought the person he was following through the steamy room was Cato and waits for his back to be turned then attacks the unarmed man by slashing his neck with a self-made knife and leaving the deceased floating face down in the water.

***

Calli and Felicia walk around the bathhouse, going into different areas as they tip toe around trying to not be caught. Felicia finally stops and says, "Wait a minute, Calli. This place is so large; we will never find your master in time. I think it is best if we go separate ways. We can cover more area that way."

Calli agrees and she and Felicia run up and down either sides of the corridors and around the steamy rooms, not able to see the hand that is in front of their face, let alone the men that are about. Calli rushes off to the left side when she finally hears moaning and laughing coming from a few of the steam rooms. Walking in the first one, she finds the prostitute on top of Anton. Calli rushes in.

"Sir Anton, please, you must help Master Cato! Your wife, Lila, and one of the guards named Brutus have planned to kill him to receive all of his property, including me! Brutus locked me in a cell and those were the words that he spoke to me!" Anton cannot believe what he is hearing. But seeing the scared look in Calli's eyes, Anton could not help but wonder. "Oh my goodness, Sir Anton! I forgot that your slave, Felicia, is here helping me look for my master!" Calli says, frantically.

Hearing this, he knows Calli cannot be lying so he stands up and both run throughout the sauna area where Cato was last, hoping he is still alive.

***

Felicia hears what seems to be a struggle between Master Cato and the two male slaves. Felicia doesn't think twice, quickly rushing over to the tub area and yanking one of the men off of him.

The male slave gets the best of Felicia, over powering her and bringing her to the floor. He then begins grabbing her hair and punching her in the face. Felicia reaches up, grabbing the guy by his scrotum and twisting and pulling as hard as she can until he falls off her. Felicia then runs over to pick up a rock to beat the slave that attacked her. The rock crumbles into small pieces; the man falls to the floor, dead.

Calli and Anton arrive to the scene just in time to witness the events while Cato and the other slave wrestled with the other handmade knife that had been planted inside a towel. Cato is able to get the knife away from his attacker, with the help of Anton wrapping a wet cloth around the slave's neck and twisting it into a tight knot while Cato punches him hard in the jaw then stabs the slave in the stomach. Anton and Cato drop the attacker, causing his dead body to collapse into the water.

Calli runs to her master and hugs him tightly. "Oh, Master Cato! I am so happy that you are unharmed! If it wasn't for this slave here, I would still be in the cell down in the slave area and who knows what would have happened!"

Cato looks over and shakes his head, still stunned that two people tried to kill him and says, "Anton, I do not know who this slave is, but she saved my life! If it was not for her, I would have died!"

Anton quickly looks up and answers, "That is Felicia! She is Lila's slave and will be in so much trouble if anyone finds out she has killed someone!"

***

The four of them arrive back to the villa. Cato and the two slaves stay in the entryway while Anton storms in and surprises Lila and Brutus, ordering his guards to arrest them both. Lila yells at her husband. "What the fuck is the matter with you? I am your wife! You cannot do this to me!"

Anton is so furious; he is shaking. He walks up to Lila, slapping her as hard as he can open handed across the face and yells, "How dare you?! You tried to have my friend killed to take all of his belongings! And you say I cannot do this! You bitch! I am doing just that! And you can rest assured it will be a very quick three days. We will allow the senate to decide on you and this guard's fate!" Anton walks back to where Cato, Calli, and Felicia are and says, "Felicia, since all of this has happened I am in fear that the other slaves will retaliate and kill you. So you will be sleeping in the guest quarters across from Cato. And Calli, I will allow you to stay in the guest room with Cato. Like I said, I do not wish to take any chances."

***

Calli and Felicia grow closer and a friendship blossoms quickly over the next three days. Anton is still in shock and cannot believe his wife would even think, let alone plan such a

112

horrid plot. The council finally made their decision. Anton goes in front of them to hear the punishment of his wife. The men did not think twice of her punishment.

A short plump bald man with large bugged brown eyes spoke up. "It has been decided by the council that Lila, wife of Anton, will be exiled to a deserted island, losing her possessions. Whether she is allowed to take one slave with her will be the decision of her husband. But, she will spend the rest of her days there." Anton and Cato are both present for the next hearing. The short bald man then spoke up again, "The council has decided on the punishment for Lila's accomplice, Brutus. The decision is that he is to suffer even worse than Lila. His punishment will be to be brutally beaten. He is to receive one hundred lashes, and the he is to be crucified!"

"If I may suggest?" Anton asks. "Brutus should not be tied to the cross, but nailed. It will be more gruesome and agonizing. His death will come more quickly! It will show to others who think of doing this what will happen when you try to plot and murder an upper classman!"

The members of council gasp, hearing this come from Anton's mouth.

Cato stands. "Apologies. I am Cato, and my father was Felix, who was in the senate. He was much respected. I am the one that was almost killed! This fucking ass, Brutus, was the one who plotted with Lila about my death and threw my slave, Calli, in a cell! I want the worst punishment known in your area for this pile of shit!"

After hearing Cato's plea, the council talks about this matter longer because this was known to be the worst form of execution. The short man appears again an hour later and says, "The council has taken everything that has been said into consideration and they will be doing the worst punishment on the known Brutus. You both may now leave."

After the exile and crucifixion of Lila and Brutus, Cato and Anton speak alone.

"My dear friend, how can I show you how sorry I am for everything that has happened? I will *do* anything, or *give* you anything."

Cato thinks quietly, and then says, "What will happen to the slave girl, Felicia, that saved my life? She did help Calli escape from the cell, saved my life in the bathhouse, bravely stood up against the two slaves who tried to murder me, and then went against her Domina. That alone would be a threat against her life."

Anton walks back and forth, looking out the window before he says, "I think of Felicia like she was my daughter. Though she is a slave, I still care for her. And she was Lila's favorite. I can see her being scorned after murdering not only one man, but helping with the two deaths, even though they were slaves and turning against her Domina. I feel she will be safer with you. If it is ok with you, would you mind watching over her? "

Cato thinks on it for a brief minute, agreeing to this arrangement. The two men go outside to tell the ladies the good news.

***

Calli sees them smiling and wonders what is going on. Bravely walking up to Cato and Anton, she asks, "Is everything ok? I do hope that Felicia is not in trouble."

Cato looks at her, running his fingers down the side of her face. "Oh, my sweet Calli, you worry too much about your Master. No need to worry yourself; all is taken care of."

Anton calls on Felicia. "With everything that has happened. I believe it is best if you go with Cato and Calli. I will pass your contract onto him. If I did not think that Cato would be fair to you, I would not be doing this. I hope you can trust me with my decision, and you are so much like a daughter to me I would hate for the citizens to learn of the murders and you turning against your Domina and them retaliating."

Felicia is saddened, but says, "Yes, I understand. But, I will miss you and hope that our paths will cross once again."

Calli is so happy that she leaps for joy, knowing now that she now has a sister. Not by blood, but they are already very close and great friends.

Anton gives Felicia a horse as a present. The horse used to belong to Lila, and he promises that he will see her again, hugging Felicia tightly. She dries her blood shot eyes as she rides away on horseback. Calli is riding behind her and Cato is on his horse on the side as the three of them ride off toward Cato's home. Felicia is so mesmerized seeing everything that they pass along the way. Seeing the falling stars once they reached the top of the hill was her favorite part. The stars look like diamonds jumping out of the sky. The moon is bright and full with no clouds. It is breathtaking and reminds Felicia of something she has seen in a dream. They hear a screech owl in the distance as it flies off to grab a mouse, and then the screeching sound of a hawk close by with it fighting with the owl for the small mouse. Felicia ducks, hearing the two birds fighting.

Cato, Calli, and Felicia finally return back to Cato's home. He shows Felicia to her room that she will be sharing with Calli for now. Felicia notices quickly how calm Master Cato is. He is a man who has a lot of patience and a kind heart. This eases her as she thinks to herself, *maybe I will be happy here at my new house and with my new sister.*

***

Cato is unable to sleep. So much has happened in the past few weeks—almost being murdered to accepting Felicia as one of his for protection.

Cato cannot help but recall the look in Calli's eyes when she saw that he was alive and unharmed. It actually made him happy and at ease with the way things were right now. He worried that if Calli were to find out how he used to be before she came in his life it just may scare her, making her want to be released from his servitude. He thinks that he is starting to fall in love with Calli. Cato looks through his papers, retrieving the scroll that is for Felicia that Anton had given him. He begins

117

pulling a few apart, being careful so as not to rip the spots that had gotten wet when the ceiling had leaked recently. He carefully picks up the scroll that is sitting tightly in a vase and places it back on his desk. He traces the red string that is a bit faded now through his fingers and stares at it. He cannot help but realize how much of a lucky man he is. Not only does he have one beautiful slave, but now he has two! He sips on his wine. *How totally lost and alone I would be if not for this precious gem that the Gods have sent to me. How do I go about telling her how I feel about her? Do I dare mention it, or just leave it how it is?* He thinks as he sits at his table going through the mounds of papers that came to him while he was away at the trial. There is no sleep tonight as there is too much to be accomplished.

But first, he walks out to his garden and thanks Apollo for allowing him to be alive. Cato walks back inside and he glances into the room where Calli and Felicia were sleeping peacefully. He smiles and walks back to his chambers.

***

Chapter 7

A month has passed and Fuscus stops by for a visit and has wonderful news to share with Cato. The news is a war from far away has finally been won! The men of their city are finally able to return home time to celebrate! Who can say no to a celebration? The city is rumbling and bustling; everyone is awaiting their soldiers to come home. All of the vendors are packed again with meats, fruits, vegetables, and bread. There is one lady in the city that makes special clothes that include jewelry. The special clothes are shear and see through, coming in an array of bright colors with small golden chains that go around the person's waist. Everyone is sure they would be having a baby boom when the husbands did return. Cato plans a large celebration for the soldiers of his city.

Everyone in the city is awoken by sounds of cheering; the men of the city have just returned from war. Everyone was celebrating a glorious victory! Calli and Felicia ready themselves for the day by putting on their best clothes, running the small leaves of honey suckles across their bodies for fragrance, and doing one another's hair. What a great day for a celebration! The wine is flowing and the cuisine is delicious. The main course consists of meat with a side of bread. There is also a dessert and, of course, fruit. After each course, the fingers are washed. The food is placed in the form of a horseshoe so the slaves could serve it more easily. There are apples, pears, and figs on one tray; carrots and olives on another tray. There is also two buckets: one filled with fish, and the other filled with squid, being held by a servant. Master Cato has invited many people to this extravagant celebration. Calli and Felicia stand by the fruit, watching the other people as they eat.

The girls start a quiet conversation amongst them as Felicia goes on saying, "Like Master Cato, my first Master was so nice. I do miss him. His name was Radix. I have not spoken of him or mentioned his name in many moons."

***

Fuscus cannot help but overhear Felicia and Calli's conversation as he leans over to tell one of the slaves to hand him a piece of meat. He dunks the meat and the bread into his wine and says in a curious tone, "How interesting. Did you say his name is Radix?" Taking a large drink out of his wine, he walks away.

***

Felicia and Calli look at each other oddly. As the celebration comes to an end and people begin to leave, Calli and Felicia make their way back to their room. Lying across the rather lumpy mat and gazing up at the stars, Felicia cannot help but notice that Calli has the better of everything. The nicest silks and dresses, hair clips, and sandals. Calli is younger than Felicia, but only by about three years. Master Cato also spends more time with Calli, as well. Felicia understands that Calli is Master Cato's first slave, and this is how some Masters are.

Many nights, Felicia stays to herself. She does not mind. Even though she does not know how to read that well, Calli is trying to teach her. She is a fast learner, too, so she has started filling her days with practicing. It is a secret between the two. Felicia reaches over and picks up a small green bound book and sounds irritated.

Calli looks up to the sound Felicia makes, asking her, "Sister, what is wrong? You should be so happy! The war is over and you are with us. And I am teaching you how to read."

Felicia flops back atop the mattress, looking up into the opened ceiling and gazing at the stars again while wiping away her tears. "Calli, I am happy to be here, and I am so happy that you are teaching me how to read. My clothes that Master Cato has bought me are very beautiful and the sandals are very comfortable; it keeps the thorns and rocks from hurting my feet and heels. My favorite part of being here is walking out to the garden any time I wish. I love the smell of the roses and other abundance of flowers that is here. But, I can't help but notice that Master spends more time with you. It just makes me sad and makes me miss my very first Master. I wonder if he is still alive. I pray that Morpheus will give me a good dream tonight."

Calli smiles and says, "I hope so, too, sister! And I do hope that Sir Radix is ok. I will ask that Apollo can answer your prayers, and someday you will find him."

Calli and Felicia talk until they both drift off to sleep.

***

In the conference room, Master Cato is speaking to Fuscus about the conversation that he overheard from Calli and Felicia earlier that night. Fuscus tells Cato of the conversation. "Cato, I know of one man that fits this description. Last I heard, he was a freeman living in the neighboring town in an Insula. I do not know if it is who Felicia speaks of, but people tell me that he lost everything and it drove him insane."

Cato clears his throat. "Did I tell you that Felicia saved my life? I am very pleased with her; she is very courageous. I do care for her. No, my house is not like Anton's and I am not like Anton either, so if she is not happy here I would be willing to let her find her old Master, but it would have to be approved of by Anton if she is to stay with this Radix. Fuscus, I want you to make sure this is the man that Felicia speaks of, and if it is, I will make arrangements to speak with both him and Anton."

Fuscus agrees to help find Radix, leaving to head home. Cato's other concern is he is not giving Felicia enough time or attention. He does try his best to spend each day with them. But with him being very busy from spending so much time at Anton's for the trials, he is starting to think that he will never finish it all. It is very early in the morning and Cato is looking through old census records, trying to find the name of Felicia's old master. Finally, he believes he has found it. Clumsily, he knocks his wine over, smudging the already frail papers even more. "Fuck! The Gods are shitting on me!" Cato is barely able to read out the name. Radix- slave- House of Quintilius. The ink smudges even more when he tries to wipe it with his hand. He is so upset with himself that he throws the papers across the room, giving a loud sigh.

***

Calli lays awake, unable to sleep. She misses her family so much, and though she is very happy to serve Master Cato, she just wanted to be able to let her family know that she is alive and well. Calli thinks of writing a letter to them, telling them of her now serving Cato and of the trips to the games that she has been on and how the people live. Will her mother and father understand? Calli worries that if they find out about how things have gone with her and how she has been treated that they would storm the gates of the city and insist to bring her back home with them. She has gotten so used to living with Cato, she does not know what she would do if she had to leave him. Calli cares deeply for him.

Calli hears Cato down the hall. She hears the many books hitting the floor and papers being scattered about. She rolls over and stares at Felicia, seeing her friend rolling all over her bed. Felicia is now her best friend. Calli then notices a small grin form across Felicia's face. Calli wonders to herself what the girl is dreaming of. It must be something wonderful to be smiling that much.

***

Felicia was having a wonderful dream indeed...*Felicia remembers one time when she was still serving Master Radix. Radix is a tall man with a big build and a tattoo across his shoulders, and big, strong hands and large, muscular legs. He had dark colored hair as dark as the night that was just below his neck, big blue eyes that were the color of the ocean that you*

could get lost in, and a strict hand but a gentle hand. He was
not difficult to please, but he did not let others know he was so
soft hearted, only showing that part to her.

Late one night, he had summoned Felicia. So, she went
to his chambers and knelt down, sitting on the heels of her feet.
She spread her legs widely across the leopard rug that was in
front of the fire pit. She waited for him patiently. Felicia knew
what was going to happen and why he had summoned her. Her
nipples hardened as the cold winter night wind blew in threw a
window. Her head bowed low and her hands placed atop her
silky smooth legs as she stared at the floor. She readied herself.
Felicia heard his footsteps outside of the chamber doors. She
ran her tongue across her pouty lips and took a large breath.
She should not be so nervous. She knew that Radix would not
be rough on her and knew what her limits were. The next thing
she knew, Radix walked in, swiftly grabbing Felicia off of the
rug and kissing her fiercely without hesitation. As he ran his
hands over her body, she felt her heart begin to race with him
pressing her against a wall. Radix leaned into her, smelling the
lilac on her soft skin and the honeysuckle that was in her
flowing blonde hair. He kissed her neck and grabbed at her
soft, round ass. She gasped as she felt his rough hands and
nails digging into her flesh. Felicia did not resist the pleasure.
She grabbed at his loosely fit trousers, determined to feel this

man inside of her; all the while tracing her tongue down his neck and tasting his flesh before biting into his shoulder.

Radix picked her up, wrapping her legs around his waist as she pressed her back against the cold, hard wall for balance. Felicia grabbed his hard cock, sliding her hands up and down and feeling it throbbing in her hand. She traced the head of it across her soft, yet dripping wet clit, barely putting the head in; just enough so he could feel how wet he made her.

She whispered in his ear, "Master, do you feel how ready I am for you? I just want to feel all of you inside of me. Please, you know this makes me want to beg for more of you, Master." She looked deep into her Master's eyes as she fluttered her eyelashes at him. Radix let out a low, raspy moan as he held her close to him, gripping harder to her ass. He tossed his head back, enjoying the pleasures she was giving him.

A candle put out just enough light to notice her beautiful features. Radix saw her hair a mess, falling in different arrays, and sweat that rolled off as small rain drops trickled down her cleavage. With one swift swoop of his hand, he pushed all the papers and maps to the floor, placing her on top of the table as he forcefully kissed her again on the mouth. He grabbed the back of her hair, forcing her head back. Radix groped one of her breasts, pinching her already hardened nipple between his fingers, and then placed it in his mouth. He playfully bit and pulled on it.

Felicia moaned low and bit her lip. She tried to remain quiet. She felt the tips of his fingers as they slowly glided down between her legs as he felt her tender wet spot. He grabbed her ankles, tossing her legs on each side as they hung off of the table. He reached over to pick up a candle. Seeing the wax and how it had trickled down on the side, he took one finger and put it inside the already hot, melted wax and traced his finger in a figure eight motion across her breast and down her cleavage, licking it off before the wax dried.

Felicia shrieks loudly. "Oh my! Yes!"

Radix gave her a small grin, noticing the wetness between her legs and how it glistens in the candle light. He leaned down to whisper in her ear. "Oh, that was just a small taste of what I have in store for you."

Radix walked around the table, searching for his rope to keep her from moving. He grabbed the rope that was wadded up and began wrapping it around Felicia's small wrists and ankles, tying each part just tight enough to not cut off the circulation, but making her immobile, and then tying each piece of the rope to the leg of the table. He took a piece of cloth, draping it over her eyes. He stood back and looked at his work. There, *he thinks to himself.* She is displayed perfectly for me. *Her being spread eagle and not being able to see is the position that made him the most aroused. He whispered in her ear calmly.* "Felicia, tell me what you hear."

Felicia is not fearful as she takes in a deep breath so as to collect her senses. "Master, I hear the crackling of the fire, the sizzling sound of the wax of the candle that sits on this table. I also hear the howling sounds of a wild animal outside close by and the blowing of the wind through the trees."

Radix replied, "Very good. Now, what do you smell?"

Felicia grew quiet before answering quickly, "The wood burning in the fire, the smell of wine that sits in the corner, the tray of figs and apples, and your scent. Your scent is that of cypress trees and burnt wood." *She smiled warmly as she said this. Radix knelt down at Felicia's feet and slightly blowed against her wetness. Felicia whimpered low, wiggling to try to get away.* "Master, may I please have more? "

Radix bent down and said in a deep voice, "You want more what? More of this?" *Taking hold of one of her breasts and squeezing it tightly, he continues. "Is this what you want, Felicia?"*

Felicia whimpered just a bit as she replied with a shaky, "N-No, Master. I want more of your hard cock deep inside of me!"

Radix noticed her juices flowing even more as she tried to ease herself closer to him. Radix grinned, pressing hard against her wetness with the palm of his hand. "Not just yet."

He made small circular motions with the tip of his tongue, starting off slow then moving faster. He could tell she was very excited and also extremely wet as his fingers glided in and out of her wet pussy. Radix leaned over and pulled the cloth off of her eyes. Felicia lifted her head as she tried to spread her legs wider. As she felt his erection pressing against her inner thigh, she arched her back and pressed herself into Radix as she felt him lean over and unties her wrists. He slipped his giant cock inside her, grabbing hold of her shoulders. Felicia let out a long, loud moan as he then grabbed her hips, working his way in and out of her, rough and hard. She dug her nails deeper into his back. She felt the blood from the scratches she had made as they trickled down her fingertips. She gave a playful grin as Radix grit his teeth, giving her a stern look as he leaned in and bit her collarbone.

129

He growled in her ear. "You are mine; everything on you is my possession! Do You Understand This?!" With each sentence, he made a hard thrust inside of her. He snapped the rope that was attached to her ankles and lifted Felicia back up by her golden wavy hair. Radix was still ramming himself deeper and harder inside of her as he looked deep into her eyes. Not losing eye contact, Felicia stared back with her blue eyes replying with a whimper that is then followed with a low moan.

"Yes, Master. Everything on me is yours."

Radix let out a roar that could awaken the Gods as he finished off inside of her. Afterward, Radix slapped her ass firmly with his hand.

Felicia awakens from her dream, still having a slight smile across her face. She then finds herself feeling sad. Felicia wonders of all people for her to dream about, why did she have to dream of Master Radix? Felicia traces her fingers against her shoulder blade; she can still feel the marking that was given to her when she served Master Radix. She did not want to wake Calli, so she decides to see if Master Cato is still awake. Felicia creeps quietly out of the room and down the long corridor and notices that the torches are still lit in Master Cato's meeting chambers.

She lightly knocks, hearing Master Cato fumbling around and grumbling before saying, "Enter."

Felicia pulls hard against the heavy door. She glances around his enormous room. Just as Calli described it; it had so many maps, papers drawings, and a large maroon rug lay in the center.

Cato looks up. "Felicia, you are still up? Is everything ok, little one?"

She looks to the floor and stumbles over her words. "Ma- Mast…Master Cato. I do not recall if I have told you yet, but… I want to thank you again for bringing me here. I promise I will not bring shame or disrespect to your name or your house." Felicia glances at the floor as Cato gives her a warm smile.

"Look at me, little one. I believe you. I still have to wonder what is on your mind. Are you sure there is not anything bothering you?"

Felicia wraps her fingers around a strand of her blonde hair as she nervously replies, "Master, I am happy to serve here and to be under your protection. But, I am curious about whatever happened to my old Dominus, Master Radix? The last I heard, he, too, was sold into slavery."

Cato glances up from his stack of papers and many books and says, "I have heard of this Radix. I heard he lost all of his possessions because he did not report it to the census. Maybe, in time, we can find what has become of him. Until then, do not worry and please get some rest."

Felicia is in shock and replies, "Yes, Master, I understand."

Felicia rushes from Cato's room, almost running to tell Calli the good news. She has a very large smile across her face. She is so happy to hear what Master Cato has told her. Felicia rushes in the bedroom where Calli still lays sound asleep. She shrieks, shaking Calli awake. "Oh, Calli! You have to wake up; I have the greatest news!"

"Ugh, what is it? Is it time to wake up already?"

Felicia giggles and says, "Well, no not really. Oh Calli, wake up, wake up! Master Cato is going to find out what happened to my old Dominus!"

Calli rubs her eyes and yawns. "That is great news, Felicia! But what if he does not remember you, or if Master Cato cannot find him?"

Felicia grabs Calli's hand, squeezing tightly. "I do hope that Radix will be found. I do not think he would have forgotten about me."

Felicia stares out the window, praying to Minerva to please answer her prayers. She is still surprised at Master Cato's response. Calli and Felicia stay up the rest of the night talking. Felicia blurts out an off the wall question. "Calli, do you love Master Cato? I know he cares for me. And I am only asking this because, well, it seems like he cares more for you than a normal Master would for his slaves."

***

Calli's eyes get big while she is trying to consider how to answer such an accusation, and after several minutes of silence says, "After everything I have gone through, Felicia, I honestly cannot answer. I mean, do I have feelings for him? Yes, I do care for Master Cato, but I do not believe it is love. After how Justus betrayed me and sold me to the auction house, I do not know how I could actually love anyone just yet." Felicia leans in, hugging her friend tightly as they both notice the rays from the sun just beginning to peak through the window.

They hear Master Cato walking through the halls, barking orders to his guards. "I do not have time to go, so you will send a guard to escort my slaves. We have received invitations, so we must make this quick! We still have to pack and ready for the trip!"

Calli and Felicia hear this and big smiles come across their faces. They are excited without hesitation as they jump from their beds and hurry around their room to get dressed. Not often do they go to the market just for new clothes. This does excite them.

Chapter 8

The two slaves are escorted by one of the guards when they go into the city. They both notice new silks that are just delivered that day and cannot help but notice that these have bracelets and anklets with bells on them. One is a teal color and the other is a light pink. They are both so excited over these items and the bracelets they have purchased.

The market is busier than usual. The mass of people pushing their way through the streets are arguing with the venders over the food prices and if the fruits were fresh enough. They hear the guard shout out loudly for the people to get out of the way. Calli and Felicia reach over and grab an orange to split and giggle amongst themselves. The guard that is escorting them rolls his eyes. Everyone can tell he is not happy at all to be babysitting two grown women. While Calli and Felicia are looking around, the guard keeps a close eye on them. Out of the corner of his eye, the guard notices a very attractive woman near a shaded building glaring at him and batting her eyes and smiling. The guard walks off, leaving the two slaves alone briefly knowing they will be alright for a short time to wander amongst themselves.

A large tent is in the middle of the market. The vendor is selling very nice rugs from the Orient that are in an array of colors and sizes, and a different kind of fruit which is known as a mango. It looks so refreshing and decadent; it makes their mouths water. The women grab a few of the interesting new fruits to take back to Master Cato. He should really enjoy them and maybe they would taste divine with his favorite fish and wine.

Just as Calli and Felicia are about to leave, they hear women shrieking in the distance followed by three Roman guards yelling for someone to "Stop!"

The large crowd turns around to see an old man running like he is cursed. He is a very skinny man. So thin, in fact, that you can see his rib cage and he has a very bloated belly. he was bald just on top of his head, but has gray hair that is sticking out in all directions, a rather long beard down to his chest, and is wearing nothing but a loin cloth. He has scrapped up knees that still have blood going down his knees and a patch like cloth over one eye. In his hand, he carries an old tree branch that he is using as a walking stick and the occasional sword as he passed by people. Some watched in shock as the man picked up different vegetables and fruits, throwing them to the crowd and cackling while running past them. Some people laugh while some gasp, standing still watching as this looney person who is acting like a wild creature refuses to be captured.

The crazy man jumps around back and forth next to Calli, dropping to his knees. Then he begins sniffing her legs like a dog and squatting down to try to lick at the Felicia's feet. Everyone in the market was noticing how frightened Calli and Felicia are by his wild look.

He stands up then gets nose to nose with Felicia and yells in a raspy, yet shriekish voice, "You! I remember you! You once served Dominus Radix until he was imprisoned! He is to fight soon, and you will see, yes, you will see that he is the greatest of all!" Hopping about still using his walking stick as a sword and making fighting stances, the man turns away from them.

Before Felicia can question the old, crazed man the three guards rush in, with one of the guards hitting the man in the face with the handle of one of their swords, and then pushing him to the ground. The three guards do not hesitate and begin hitting the old man atop his head with their heavy shields and kicking him about his entire body as hard as they can, the sound of his head being crushed between the shield and the ground echoing through the crowd. Calli and Felicia cover their eyes and try to turn their backs, hearing the agonizing screams the man makes with the heavy feet of the Roman guards kicking his thin, old, frail body. The man tries to stand up, but one guard strikes him hard with a running kick to the man's temple which makes him fall to his death. Bruises that have already formed are visible against his skin and wounds are covering his body. The guards pick the man up and carry him away.

Calli and Felicia are so startled with what just happened, the two did not notice a very tall man that was watching them very closely and sees the small basket that Felicia has sat down at her feet. The man passes by and drops a small object into her basket then walks away quickly before he is noticed. The guard that is supposed to be watching Calli and Felicia hears the chaos and quickly runs back to check on the outcome. The guard turns around to see the sun just setting on top of the mountains.

"We better start heading back before it gets too late. Dominus will not be happy if we are out at nightfall," the guard says.

The tall man that was watching them earlier glides by Felicia, giving both of the ladies a warm smile and handing them each a mango before walking past and turning around to bow to them. "What beautiful ladies you both are. Whoever your owners are must be very proud to have you lovelies wear their collars."

Calli and Felicia look at each other, giving the man a small smile but do not reply. The guard walks up to the man and shoves him. "These slaves serve the house of Felix and are owned by Dominus Cato. Any problems you have with them may be noted and will be sent to him."

The man's eyes grow large, hearing this information. He bows again. "My apologies," the man says before turning and walking away.

Calli and Felicia look at each other in shock as that has never happened before. The two women do not respond and just look at the ground while making their way back to the villa. Calli looks over at Felicia, who was still munching away at her mango. She notices a deep scar of a small circle that has a RX in the center of it on Felicia's shoulder. The scar has faded, but is still legible enough for Calli to understand that it must have been the marking of Felicia's old Master, Radix. Calli remembers when the guards tried to brand her. The smell of her flesh and hair burning made her nauseous even now. The pain was more than she could handle, making her pass out.

Calli, Felicia, and the guard finally make it to the villa and walk past the meeting room. Calli and Felicia can hear Cato speaking with someone. They overhear the faint conversation—something about tickets and games. Could it be the Gladiator games? Maybe it was thieves being fed to the lions? Could it possibly be a skit that is being played by the Christians?

Calli and Felicia walk to their room to put away their new clothes. Felicia reaches in her small basket and feels an object that she had not purchased, unwrapping it slowly to see it is a small silver heart locket. On one side, it looks like a bird cage with a small heart inside of it. This necklace looks like something from a fairytale, and on the back it says, *"Te Amo"* which means 'love'. It has a white ribbon tied through it and a tiny key attached to it. Felicia stands in astonishment as she looks at this gorgeous item that she holds in her hand. Calli looks at Felicia, who is all but crying, and has to go over to investigate why her sister is so upset. She notices the beautiful possession. "Oh, Felicia! It is so pretty! When did you get this?" she asks.

Felicia looks up, still surprised, and says, "I don't know. I found it in my basket wrapped up underneath my silks! But isn't it breathtaking, Calli?! I think it is, and I am going to

140

carry this with me everyplace I go. I believe it is a sign of good things to come. Calli sees the words on the back. She looks at Felicia, confused. "What does that mean? I am still learning your language."

Felicia smiles and says, "Love."

Calli squeals with excitement from what her sister has found and exclaims, "Oh Felicia, how romantic! I have a great idea. You can bunch that up and pin it to the inside of your dress for when we go to the games with the holiday coming up!"

***

The holiday that Calli was speaking of has finally come. And Cato is speaking to Fuscus. "Tell me, Fuscus, did you find the man that was once Felicia's owner?"

"No, I have not. Not yet, but I will be going to the neighboring town tomorrow. I will hope to see you and the girls there as well."

Cato nods his head. "Yes, the three of us will be attending the games. I have informed Calli and Felicia, and they both sound thrilled."

"That's great!"

"I need your opinion, Fuscus. Have you ever heard of a man of my stature falling in love with a slave?"

"Well, I guess it can happen. It is rather frowned upon, though. Why; who have you fallen in love with? Is it Calli or Felicia?"

Cato grins at his friend and says, "I will not be answering that last question. I will see you at the games." Calli and Felicia walk to the conference room and kneel, waiting for Cato to exit. It was a few hours but he finally came out and notices them both kneeling. "I would have thought that you both would be in bed by now; it is late and we have a very busy day tomorrow."

Calli stands up, handing Cato the newly found fruit and then giving him a light kiss on his cheek.

Felicia stands, handing him a piece of kiwi and then hugging him lightly. They both turn and skip off to bed. Cato stands, watching them both. *What was that?* he thought, looking down at the interesting looking fruits and glancing back up with a warm smile forming across his face.

Just like Cato promised, him, Calli, and Felicia head to the games. They arrived early so Cato could see the parade of the fighters. He listens carefully, hearing what the fighters' names and skills are so he can be able to decide on who he thinks is a winner. He watches closely as the fighters walk through the streets. He had to decide on who looked the strongest. There were ten fights that day. He looks on a wall, noticing some of the recent drawings. Cato holds on to the tickets that he received from Fuscus. Cato is not surprised at the commotion. He stands back, watching as Calli and Felicia glare at the many items hanging across the walls. Calli and Felicia look through the stalls, seeing the many souvenirs they have on sale that day. One vender has clay figures of the gladiators that are fighting that day, oil lamps, knives, and other interesting items.

Felicia picks up a small clay figure and turns to Calli. "Sister, this little figurine looks like my old master; only this has a beard and long hair."

"Felicia, are you sure? Because that is not how I would picture Radix."

Felicia places the clay statue back and says, "You're right. Why would he be here?"

They both head back to where Master Cato is waiting and they all enter the Amphitheater just in time. The seats are not the closest to the ring, but they are close enough to get a great view. They sit in the area across from the emperor. Of course, the emperor has the best seats. He was right in front.

***

Cato sits in his chair with Calli and Felicia sitting on each side of his feet. The events for the day started as per usual: Animal hunts in the morning with exotic animals that fight one another—this day they had elephants and bulls. Sometimes, these animals were so scared that men would have to chase them down with spears just so they would actually fight with the gladiators. That match was over within thirty minutes. It took a while for the men to get the wild animals back in the cages, but when that match was over it was followed by the criminal executions. This is when all of the criminals are hoarded out like animals in the middle of the arena and given swords, and are then told to reenact a scene from a battle. The last criminal standing would be the winner and allowed to live. He would then be given the chance to be taken back to the ludus and be taught on how to become a gladiator.

Today's afternoon entertainment would begin with a comedy fight. When the trumpets would sound off, it meant that it was finally time for the gladiators to have a warm up fight. A parade of men carry the extremely heavy weapons and bulky armor for the gladiators.

At times, the gladiators would fight naked, or in loincloths. The gladiators march into the arena as the audience stamped their feet with excitement and cheered loudly. These fights can last anywhere from a few minutes up to fifteen minutes. No one in the audience would leave their seat in fear of losing it. So if they had to relieve themselves, they would do so where they sat.

***

Felicia and Calli watched as the two gladiators practiced their warm up fight. The two women look around and see the wealthy men with their pretty companions, some women but others men. Felicia tilts her head up at the higher towers above them. She notices a woman offering herself from the rear of her partner so they can both watch the games. The more experienced prostitutes discreetly sucked their partner off during the carnage and would be able to bring them off at the very moment of the kill. Calli was in shock from that. She looks at the level below her, and she notices a woman who is not one bit shy. This woman has nasty looking brown hair that is up in a bun. The woman opens her robe, fully exposing her small but perky white breasts and her vagina to the gladiators as they make their way around the arena. Her husband, who is aroused by his wife's bold moves, grabs her and sits her on his lap so the other people above and next to him could see as his hard cock entered her pussy. Another woman is sitting beside the couple, and she thinks that she can get the attention of the Gladiators by sitting on the ledge with her legs spread wide as she removes her robe and leans back, posing for all to see her rather large breasts and perky nipples. She sits up, waving her hand frantically at the gladiators who cannot help but laugh. The woman's husband reaches up and yanks his wife down before she falls, pushing her against the awning and then entering her hard from behind.

Calli looks over to the people who are sitting on the side of her. The couple can be heard laughing and moaning as the young lover is chained to the chair and his partner makes her suck him off. Calli cannot help but be turned on by all the sex that is going on around her. She glances up, noticing Cato intrigued by the fight and paying no mind to everything going on around him. Calli cannot help but get very aroused by all of this. Cato is still focused on the fight, so she places one finger inside her mouth and gets it soaking wet then begins tracing her fingers along the opening of her pussy. The more sounds that the crowd makes, the more Calli fingers herself. Cato glances down, noticing Calli in a hypnotic state. Her eyes are

146

closed tight and her mouth is half open. He taps Felicia on the shoulder as he points at Calli.

***

Cato leans down and whispers in Calli's ear, "If you are going to do that here, you will open your legs."

Calli glances up and whispers, "Yes, Master."

Doing as she is told, she leans back against the wall and stretches her legs out then places her fingertips over her g-spot, tracing them back and forth. Felicia slides over, straddling Calli as they sit on the floor. She traces her hand across Calli's face, moving the hair away from her eyes. Felicia leans in, giving Calli a long, slow, passionate kiss. Calli is surprised at Felicia's action, but slowly opens her eyes and closes them again, responding with an even deeper kiss. Placing her hands on Felicia's breast, she nuzzles them against her face and tightly squeezes them. The women both release low moans, and Felicia pulls Calli's head back to tracing her tongue across her neck, nipping and pulling with her teeth when she comes to her earlobe. Her mouth waters as she hears the whimpering sounds leave Calli's mouth. She smiles as she feels Calli begin to grind her wetness into hers. Hearing the crowd's loud applauses, Felicia spins around to face the game. She licks the palm of her hand, placing it against Calli's wetness and moving her palm from front to back, slightly swatting her. She hears Calli let out a low moan as Felicia shifts her weight, pushing her wet pussy toward Calli's. The two women begin grinding their wetness into each other. Calli crawls slowly behind Felicia, dragging her teeth down Felicia's spine, kissing the back of her neck, and tracing her tongue across Felicia's shoulder. Felicia trembles as she feels the tip of Calli's tongue being drugged slowly down across her body. Calli takes her hand, grabbing a hand full of Felicia's hair and yanking her head back. She whimpers and moans in Calli's ear, begging for more and not wanting her to stop.

Cato sits in amazement and shock as he watches these women and can feel his cock getting harder and throb. The faster they move, the louder the two get. He cannot keep himself from grabbing Calli and placing her on his lap. She groans loudly when she feels Cato's very hard cock entering her. Cato pushes down on Calli's shoulders, pushing himself deeper inside of her. Felicia crawls on her knees and places her elbows on the brick of the awning with her ass sticking in the air, bouncing it back and forth with her legs spread wide and then sliding down into the splits and arching her back with her feet against the wall. Looking back, she sees Cato's cock swiftly going in and out of Calli's pussy. Tracing her hands

148

over her breast and grabbing at her nipples, she forces her three fingers deep inside of her with her other hand rubbing her g-spot in a small circle then letting out a loud moan as her hand fills with liquid.

Cato's mouth drops seeing Felicia bringing her own self to orgasm. He removes Calli from his lap and quickly wipes himself off with his robe then grabs Felicia from the floor, leaning her against his chest. He slowly kisses her bare back and shoulders, sliding her hands to his sides and placing his strong hands gently between her thighs to pry her legs wide open.

Calli leans down and begins to slowly blow against Felicia's wetness, tracing her tongue across her slit and then slowly buries her face deep into Felicia's wetness. Felicia lets out a muffled groan as Cato slaps her ass, ordering Felicia to grind hard against Calli's face at one point. Felicia reaches down with one hand, grabbing Calli by her bangs and moving her head back and forth as her other hand caresses her breast. Calli can taste Felicia's wetness as she sticks her tongue deeper inside. Calli traces her tongue across her mouth, letting out small moaning sounds when she looks up and notices her friend grab Master Cato's giant cock, placing it deep inside her mouth. Felicia's head bobbing up and down and tracing her tongue across the tip of his cock that has just started to cum. She flings her head back, moaning loud and feeling Calli crawl just underneath her and slowly placing two fingers inside of her, wiggling them back and forth at the same time. Calli places the tip of her tongue barely across Felicia's slit. It is too much for Felicia to take and she tries to wiggle out of the way like a fish out of water as fast as she can, but before she can Cato grabs her shoulders and pushes her head down onto him.

***

Calli moves her hips in small circles as she traces her hands across her bare flesh, feeling her body heat rise with even more excitement as she feels Felicia's hips grinding slowly with the motions she is making and her mouth that is also in sync, having Cato's swollen cock inside her warm mouth. Felicia and Cato both stop and look at Calli, who is still under Felicia.

Cato and Felicia both give Calli a devious smile, deciding to make sure that Calli has an orgasm that she will never soon forget. Felicia spins around, pushing Calli against the wall then bends down, gripping Calli's thighs and making sure her legs are spread eagle as wide as they can go. She begins to rub her fingers across Calli's gentle area as Felicia glides the tip of her tongue across Calli's wet lips, pulling them open with the palms of her hands and slowly kissing Calli's wetness while lightly licking. Calli feels her eyes begin to roll in the back of her head; arching her back when she feels Felicia placing her fingers deep inside of her.

Cato positions himself behind Felicia, teasing her wet pussy with the head of his cock then hearing Felicia moan when he slides his hard cock inside of her, and grasping her hips and plunging himself deep inside of her, rocking his hips back and forth while slapping her ass—hard. Felicia whimpers. She feels Calli dripping with excitement. Cato watches and pushing himself deeper into Felicia, seeing Calli lying across the floor and biting her lip while moaning and begging for Felicia to stop, her lifting her hips and grinding herself into Felicia's mouth. Cato grips hold of Felicia's hair, each thrust harder than the last. He lets out an orgasmic shutter just as the match is ending, Calli and Felicia following with an orgasmic shutter as the three orgasm together in queue; Calli's orgasm the hardest. The three gain their composure as they hear the sounds of trumpets roaring throughout the stadium, giving queue to all that the big match was about to begin.

As a surprise, there would be two big matches for the day. The first sound of trumpets sounded off to give the gladiators time to get in position as they are ready to come out

151

of the iron gates. This match had a Velites. Velites fighters had a spear that is specially made for them and is attached to a long strap. It could be pulled quickly so the gladiator can toss it over and over again. He would fight gladiators that are the same as him. They have to be fit and show the same strength. The two men started off throwing their spears at one another. The one gladiator caught his opponent as the spear went into his shoulder blade just below the skin. The blood shoots out as the opposing man screams in horror. The audience cheers loudly as the other Velites yanks his spear back then catches it in his hand, tossing it again quickly at his opponent, who is on his knees.

The Velites roll across the dirt, scrambling to his feet and running quickly toward his opponent with his weapon in hand and making stabbing motions. This time it scrapes his opponent's thigh. The next toss penetrates the man's foot as he screams in more pain; the crowd cheers as he is limping. Calli and Felicia watch as the two men grow tired, but neither are giving up. The man with the most wounds starts to run for his spear that is farther away than he had thought. As he quickly bends down to grab his weapon, his opponent throws his spear at him. The crowd gasps as it goes straight through his throat. The loser falls in a puddle of blood as the people in the stands cheer. Calli watches in horror as the crowds scream loudly, wanting to make sure the man is dead. The winner is handed a hot iron that he would poke his dead opponent with. The smell of the burning flesh was horrible, making her sick of her stomach. Calli is in utter shock of the outcome. This was nothing like her parents would do.

***

Felicia hides her eyes and covers her mouth. She recalls having to help get rid of the dead gladiators when she was serving Anton and Lila. To make sure the gladiators were dead, they would take them out of the arena and then cut the dead man's throat. The worst thing she recalled having to do was climbing the stands to clean the feces and other body fluids off of the seats. Felicia would rather pour fresh sand over the pools of blood or pick up the body parts than have that job. She cringes and gags as she remembers this.

The trumpets sound off again. The Amphitheater is a roar of screaming people rooting and cheering for their favorite gladiator. The two men come out quickly, and Calli and Felicia watch as the two men try to impress the audience with their special fighting skills. This last match was a Retiarri – this gladiator fights with a net and spear that has three tips called a trident. His armor was on his left arm and shoulder. He would try to capture his enemy in the net before he is attacked.

Retiarris were trained to fight gladiators called Secutores or "CHASERS"; they wore special helmets with very small eye holes that could stop them from being stabbed in the face with the Trident. The gladiators would fight until it was very clear that one of them was going to win. If they both impressed the crowd with their skills, they might be allowed to live. Felicia watches as she notices the Secutores move quickly as he makes stabbing gestures with his short sword to the Retiarii. The Retiarii jumps in the air on his way down and hits the chaser with the handle of his triton; blood splatters across the dirt as the Chaser stabs the Retiarii just above the knee with his small sword and then slices his face across the cheek bone. The Chaser bolts across the arena in a zigzag motion, and the Retiarii grips his net tightly, tossing it in the air and watching it fall over his opponent.

Felicia watches as she sees a resemblance in the moves that the chaser has. She cannot help but remember her training from her days as a female gladiator that was at the ludus—the men and the very few women that were allowed had to swear an oath that they could be burnt, chained, and beat when being trained. The teachers are also very successful gladiators. Felicia is snapped back into reality when she hears the crowd boo and chant, "Kill him, kill him!"

***

The Retiarii looks at the emperor waiting for him to give his decision. The emperor is so impressed by both fighters that he gives a thumbs up, which allowed both of the men to live. The crowd cheers as the two gladiators walk back to the gates to their areas. Cato, Calli, and Felicia wait until they are almost the last ones to leave. The people were leaving and heading back to their homes. The streets are filled with the crowds from the games waiting to see the gladiators who fought today. Plus, there are many prostitutes still hanging around the amphitheater, trying to get attention by the winners of the day's matches. The ladies all but threw themselves at the Gladiators. Cato, Calli, and Felicia exit the amphitheater carefully while watching for thieves. Cato knew that right after the games they loved to rob people, so he escorted Calli and Felicia and the three walked cautiously to Lucius house.

***

An older man that works at one of the stalls notices Cato, Calli, and Felicia heading to the house that is just above the ludus. As the three walk by, he cannot help but notice Felicia's marking on her shoulder. The clerk then walks up to Felicia and says with a smile, "With the okay of your Dominus, I would like to give you this clay figurine as a gift! It is the last one I have." Cato smiles, thanking the gentleman and paying him for the small statue.

***

Felicia smiles, thanks him, and wishes him well. She thinks it was odd that the man gave her his last clay figuring. Fuscus is there as well. He is visiting Lucius; who gave the tickets away. The couple invited Fuscus, Cato, Calli, and Felicia to stay for dinner. Calli and Felicia are allowed to sit and eat with Cato. This surprised Fuscus and Cato. Camilla was normally not this nice to slaves. She was fair to her own, but even they would only be allowed to eat in the kitchen. While they are eating, Camilla notices the old marking on Felicia.

Camilla clears her throat and says, "You, new slave of Cato, what house did you serve under, and when?"

Felicia gives a small smile then looks up, quietly replying, "Well, Domina, I once served Master Radix. But, he was sold into slavery; it was a very long time ago. I now serve under Master Cato. I am pleased to be under his house."

Camilla glances over to Lucius while taking a drink of her wine and says, "I have not heard of him."

Calli and Felicia retrieve the dishes, bringing them to the other slaves to clean. They notice a glimpse of a red haired slave going through the opposite door to serve the gladiators.

Cato, Calli, and Felicia leave to head home and Camilla asks Cato, "I could not help but notice you and your two slaves really enjoying one another at the games today. "

"Yes we did. Why do you ask?"

Camilla shakes her head with a grin. "How would you feel if one of your slaves was introduced to her old Master?"

Cato stops, staring at Camilla. "I would allow her to see him but under careful eye. Why? Do you know where Radix is?" He asks.

Camilla gives a loud chuckle and says, "Maybe I do. Maybe I don't. Or just maybe he is here at the ludus. If you come back in one week, there will be another round of games. He may be fighting that day."

Cato glances over, noticing how happy Calli and Felicia look. He nods to Camilla and then says, "Yes; we will be here for the next games. Thank you, and we will see you in one week."

He notices Fuscus up the hill so he calls out to him. Fuscus waves his hand. Cato tells Calli and Felicia to go on ahead and he will catch up. He has to talk to Fuscus. Cato says to Fuscus, "I talked to Camilla and I tell you she is very confusing."

"Were you able to find any information on the man you spoke of, Fuscus? Was the man Radix?"

"I found the man, but sadly it is not him. The man I found was too old; he could be Felicia's father. Did Camilla say she would help you find out if this Radix is in her house?" Fuscus asks.

Cato chuckles. "Well, she did not tell me much just yes, no, maybe, maybe not. I swear, women can be so confusing. However, she did tell me to show up at the next games and Radix may or may not be there."

***

Fuscus rolls his eyes and laughs. "I did get the tickets for the next games." Fuscus hands three tickets to Cato out of his bag.

Almost nearing their homes, Calli, Felicia, Cato, and Fuscus stop to rest. It is so hot and to make it worse they were

158

walking into a sand storm. After letting the storm pass, they notice more crosses just outside of the city. They notice the council of their city has crucified even more people. These are mostly thieves and adulterers. The four cover their mouths with their cloaks, trying to ignore the stench of the already rotting flesh that lingers in the air. Finally, they are pleased to be returning home. But the week goes by quickly and before they knew it they are reading themselves again for the journey. Earlier in the morning they are to leave for the games. Cato and Fuscus walk into the meeting room to discuss it, and Fuscus questions, "Maybe Lucius knows, since it is his ludus?"

Cato shakes his head. "I am not going to ask Lucius that question. He would think I am out to steal one of his gladiators. I guess we will have to wait and see."

***

Cato tells Calli and Felicia to go to the bathhouse. Calli and Felicia pay their fee, walk in, stripping their clothes and handing them to the attendant. The attendant hands them each a small bottle of scented infused oil and a towel. Calli and Felicia enter the gym area where they did some exercises, working up a sweat. Then they make their way to the, caldarium. They lay in the warm water as they enjoy the aroma of oranges, lavender, and chamomile. Felicia and Calli take turns washing

159

and rinsing each other. The women rub sand and oil over each other's body and massage it in. The attendant is curious when hearing the two giggle and tease one another. She sneaks in, peaking over the column. Calli traces her hands across Felicia's breast, gently squeezing them she leans in and sucks on Felicia's nipple. Felicia groans low and arches her back. Felicia glides her hands down Calli's curvy body, taking her fingertips and tracing them across her waist and brushing against her wetness. Calli glances at Felicia as she leans in and glides her tongue across Felicia's lips.

***

The attendant is shocked to see this. Felicia slides down the step of the tub, motioning for Calli to come beside her. Calli sways through the warm waters, sitting next to her friend. They each mirror the other as they touch themselves passionately as they each scoop up small handfuls of water and splash it against their sex. Felicia slides over, kissing Calli on her mouth and neck, and then gliding her tongue across her chest and flicking it over Calli's hard nipples. Calli runs her hands through Felicia's hair, lifting her chin as she kisses her deeply then presses her face down her body.

As Calli lies on her back, moaning and rubbing her fingers across her pussy, she glances up and looks at Felicia and gives her a warm smile. Felicia spreads Calli's legs as they fall open over her shoulders as she bends down on all fours and leans in to kiss Calli gently on the mouth. She inserts her fingers slowly inside of her, rotating them in a circular motion and tracing the tip of her tongue down Felicia's cleavage, stomach, and inner thigh. She lifts Felicia's legs and gives her a grin before spreading her legs and crawling between them as she presses her tongue against Felicia's slit. Calli arches her back, moving back and forth with her tongue tracing along the sides. Felicia lifts her head and arches her back, moaning louder and begging for more.

***

The two stand up, kissing each other forcefully and then making their way toward the sauna room. Felicia stops for a brief moment as she feels Calli's wetness dripping across her fingers. Felicia lies back on the bench, telling Calli to straddle herself over Felicia's face. Calli's barely standing on her the tips of her toes. She tries rotating her hips and not lose her balance. Felicia places her hands over Calli's waist, pulling her tightly on top of her. Calli lets out an echoing moan, gripping at her breasts tightly as Felicia's tongue flicks across her clit. She feels her legs begin to shake uncontrollably with a sudden rush of ecstasy going through out her entire body. Calli slides off Felicia and digs her nails deep into the wooden bench.

Felicia sits up in a rather bratty mood when she sees Calli standing up from the bench. She reaches back and slaps Calli hard across her ass, making it sting. "Hey! I was not even close to finished with you yet!" Then she reaches over and pinches Calli's buttocks.

Felicia laughs as she watches Calli fall to the floor and screech, "Ouch! I thought I was going to lose my breath and I could not take it anymore, Felicia! That was better than at the Amphitheater," she said while catching her breath. They glance at each other and smile. Calli and Felicia both wash off their sweat and rinse in the cool water. They make their way to the changing area, redress, and then head back home.

***

Cato hears the giggles as Calli and Felicia enter. He hears them laughing and walks out, giving them a warm smile. Cato tells them they needed to already have left for the games. It was a few hours travel time. This time the journey was not bad. There was a nice, relaxing breeze that was coming in from behind them, so they did not notice the humidity. The three enter the city and find it even busier than last week. The shops were so busy there were people standing outside of the tents waiting to see what they had left to purchase. Cato hears the parade just beginning. He tells Calli and Felicia to go ahead and look around while he decides to walk over to see who would be fighting today. Hearing the young man yelling out the names and strengths of the gladiators, Cato places his bets. Cato feels confident that he will win.

After the parade and shopping, Calli and Felicia go to Lucius and Camilla's villa. Cato has to speak to Lucius and Camilla regarding the games. Lucius is surprised to see Cato arriving so early, but of course welcomes him once again to his home as their honorary guest, stepping out to the balcony to watch the gladiators practice.

Cato looks down to the gladiators and asks Lucius, "I have been informed that you may have a gladiator that I am searching for?"

"I have many Gladiators. You know this and you have gladiators, too, that fight here as well. They have made you a lot of coin the pass few fights; you would be proud. Do you wish to trade one of yours for mine?"

Cato shakes his head. "No, I do not wish to trade you Gladiators. And I am very proud of all of the men who fight for me. I am wanting to know if you have a gladiator who resides in these walls named Radix."

Lucius' nostrils begin to flare as he begins shaking his finger at Cato and shouts, "Now see here: Camilla told me you would question me on Radix! She told me that you were wanting him. He is one of my best gladiators and brings in the most coin for me. People come from the other cities just to see him. He is more loved that Jupiter himself. And Achilles would have wanted to fight beside him if given the chance!"

Calli and Felicia stay in the entry way, both kneeling patiently while waiting on Cato. They try their best to glance at the floor, but they can't help but notice many of the slaves that are cleaning, cooking, and prepping for the big evening. There is always a very large gathering and celebration after the games. They see the fish and squid being placed in the silver buckets, and then the buckets are placed on top of water to keep them cold. The fruit is sliced and placed on platters and then put on fancy cloth. There are two slaves that are standing nude and being scrubbed down with oil and sand then have water poured over them. These two slaves are going to be human trays and have the deserts placed across certain parts of their bodies. Their hair is braided tightly and is then placed in a circular shape.

One slave walks by, carrying giant vases of wine and placing each vase at a table and the main table where the owners will be seated. She walks back by Calli and Felicia and sees the marking across Felicia's shoulder. It catches her curiosity as she quietly walks over to Felicia and questions her, "Hey you, blonde girl of Sir Cato. There are rumors that your Dominus is looking for one of the Gladiators whose name is Radix?"

Felicia glances over and whispers quietly, "Yes, this is true. Why do you know of him? Does he reside in these walls?"

The slave chuckles, giving Felicia a dirty look. "Yes, I know of him, silly girl. Why do you think I came here and asked you that question? He lives here in this ludus. He visits the Domina in her quarters frequently. That is her lover. We all know he is her favorite."

Felicia's eyes fill with tears. She is so hurt and drops her head in her hands and weeps. Calli tries consoling her sister as she gives an evil look to the other slave. Camilla can be heard in the other room screaming at the slaves as they rush to try to ready her for the games. In the next room, Lucius and Cato can be heard.

Lucius looks through the doors, seeing the slaves have stopped working and yells, "What the fuck? Why did you stop working? Get back to work, or I will sell the lot of you to the meanest owner I can find!"

Cato replies, "Apologies, but I told my slave I would look into what happened to him. I had read that he used to be very wealthy and he was Felicia's Master at one time. She still has his marking."

Lucius shakes his head and shouts, "I am aware of who he USED to be! Then, he got greedy and did not turn in all of his info for the Census. That is how he got into this predicament. He fights for me now and he is bringing in a lot of money! Now you know of him and you can tell your slave girl, Felicia, this! I do not know if I will allow him to fight today now."

Cato nods his head, agreeing with Lucius. "Apologies, my friend. I am not here to argue. I do not want your gladiator; I am not meaning to disrespect you in your house or in front of your slaves. We will go to the Amphitheater now." Cato walks into the entry way, taking Calli and Felicia and making their way to the Amphitheater.

Cato, Calli, and Felicia walk past a stall and the ladies look at the souvenirs, noticing the different clay figurines in their fighting positions, painting on walls, and more lamps. Felicia looks at the owner and says, "I was here last week. You gave me the last statue of a gladiator. I appreciate the gift. But, may I ask why you did this?"

The old man looks at Felicia and smiles. "Do you not know who he is? Why, he is the strongest and most popular. He may be stronger than Appolo." The old man chuckles as he goes on. "Yes, I do remember seeing this fighter. He fought a bull and a bear his first fight. The Gods have blessed this man."

Calli and Felicia notice all the prostitutes that linger around the gladiator area that is fenced in and Cato walks up to the guarded area. "Do any of you know a gladiator named Radix?"

The men look at him and chuckle. A man walks out of the shadows and says, "I know of this Radix that you speak of. He is my brother; we were both sold to the same ludus. Why? Who are you? What is your name?"

Cato pauses before speaking. "My name is Cato and I live in the city across from here."

The man says, "I have not heard of you, but I will tell my brother that you are asking of him."

Cato replies back, "I will cheer for both your brother and for you. And I wish you the best of luck."

The gladiator laughs. "We do not need luck; we are gladiators!"

The man walks back sitting down in the shaded area. The guards open the gates for the crowd of people to be seated. The line is long and it is more humid that day than the last time they were there. The man standing in from of them has two slaves, a man about 19 years of age and a female that is around 18 years old. They are being drugged around by a thick chain like a dog. Calli and Felicia cannot help but feel sorry for them and are thankful that Master Cato does not do that to them. The female slave apparently can't speak, making it hard for her owner to understand what she wants. She makes hand motions, cupping her hands under her chin and lifting them up to her mouth as she makes a loud grunting noise. Thankfully, the male slave can understand what she wants and informs their master that she wants a drink.

Their master yells at the lady. "Wait until we get seated! I am not losing my spot because you have a thirst!"

Calli remembers she still has a small bottle of water that she filled from the waterfall and a piece of fruit. She leans over to Cato. "Master Cato, I still have a bottle of water and pieces of fruit from our trip here. Would you think those slaves master would mind if I gave these items to them?" Cato gives Calli a warm smile and then kisses her on top of her forehead. "You are a very caring woman, my sweet Calli. Hand me the small bag and I will ask him."

Calli looks at Felicia and smiles. Then hands the tote to Cato, who then walks over to the man. "Apologies, sir, but I could not help but over hear your slaves are wanting drink and food. I do have a small bottle and three pieces of fruit that will surly parish in this humidity if not eaten soon. Would you and your slaves care for them?"

The man looks at Cato in surprise. Most men do not just hand over their food and drinks without a price or other reasons. "Oh, thank you, sir, but I have no coin to pay for those. I have already paid all of my coin for the tickets and I am hoping to make it back and then some at the games."

Cato looks down at the two very hungry and thirsty slaves, noticing they are without a doubt thirsty and look like they will both parish if not given food soon. Cato then hands the bag of water and the three pieces of fruit to their owner and says, "I cannot take any coin for these, as they did not cost me anything. The water is fresh and clear from my waterfall and it will quench your thirst, and the fruit is purchased at our market back home. They are a new fruit known as a mango. They are very delicious and will fill your tummies."

The man is very thankful for the gift and thanks Cato repeatedly for them.

Cato smiles, knowing deep down he has done something good for the day at least.

Calli and Felicia make their way into the amphitheater and find their seats. They get seated just in time to watch as men put on a reenactment of a sex show, mocking the god, Apollo. After that is over, they bring the thieves in to fight the tigers with wooden swords.

The crowd cheers, screams, and laughs at the men in the arena as they are eaten by the ferocious creatures. Calli feels her stomach begin to jump around. She feels ill and dizzy. Searching in her bag, she finds small pieces of ginger root that she had bought from the market. The lady that she bought it from told her that it would help heal tummies from jumping around and if she would add the small pieces of the ginger root to the water and the mint it would be like a magic spell going on inside of her.

Calli looks up to the sky as she feels the heat of the sun beating down on top of her. She looks over to the arena to see all the blood and carcasses strung about the walls. She catches the strong odor of the bodily fluids that are coming in and circling around her. Calli feels so sick that she leans her head over on top of Cato's knee. Calli closes her eyes, trying to make the world stop spinning. She starts to feel a little better until she opens her eyes to see the horrid sight in front of her. She takes in a small breath of air, hoping that will help. It didn't. It made it worse and she almost gets sick from the sight of the blood that has saturated the sand. Cato traces his hand across Calli's head and feels how clammy she feels. He leans down. "Are you ok, Calli?" he asks her.

Calli looks up at him with her pale sickly look. "No, Master. I am not well at all. I feel like I am being punished for something. Can you please hand me the small bottle of water in the bag? And there are small pieces of what the healer called Ginger root; she says it will help heal my aching tummy."

"Of course, but do not let those around us see you mixing this as they will think you are doing something wicked." Cato hands Calli the items and she soon begins to sip on the ginger and minted tasting water. She finds a small piece of bread that is very crunchy. Breaking the crunchy bread off, she takes small bites.

Cato can tell that Calli is sick. He picks her up from the floor and cradles her in his arms. He tries to shield the rays of the sun from her body. The humidity is making her even more faint. She hides her face in Cato's chest. Felicia leans up, glancing over to Calli and noticing tears trickling down her face. Felicia quickly grabs a lightly colored piece of fabric from her bag and drenches it with water then wraps it across Calli. Calli then starts to feel better, but drifts off to sleep in her Masters arms.

Felicia leans over to comfort her friend. "Oh, Master Cato. I hope Calli will soon feel well."

Cato looks at Calli and worries as well. "I am sure the wet fabric you put across her will help tremendously. I never thought to do that. I will let her sleep. I do not want to disturb her and will let her sleep where she is." The next thing they heard was the loud sound of the crowd's cheers, stamping their feet and followed with clapping their hands for their favorite fighter. The gladiators for the last match are a Thraeces; they are named after the Thracian tribe. These fighters only wear their protection on their sword arms, a small shield that is shaped like a rectangle, and curved swords. The helmets are decorated with a Griffin. A creature that the Romans believe guard the dead. The Thraeces is fighting against the Hoplomachi. His armor is similar to the Thraeces armor. He also uses a rectangular shield and fights with a sword or a spear. The Hoplomachi throws the spear early on in the fight and will fight the rest with his sword. They also looked like one of Rome's old enemies; the Greek hoplite soldiers. This is where the name Hoplomachi came from.

Cato has no idea which fighter is Radix or his brother. He cheers for both men, which is odd. But, Cato did not care. The Hoplomachi runs out of the gate with his giant spear gripped tightly in his left hand and his sword in his sheath. The Thraces walks out slowly and he stands firmly in place. The Hoplomachi throws his spear as hard and straight as he can. The Thraces ducks with the spear hitting the wall behind him as he runs up with his sword. The Hoplomachi draws his sword out of his sheath, screaming at his enemy while swinging his sword over his head. The Thraces lifts his shield in time as his opponent's sword connects with it. The crowd cheers and boos as their favorite gladiator fights his own way.

Camilla and Lucius both smile and point at the fighters below.

Cato leans over and whispers to Felicia, "I think Radix is down there fighting! Look…" she exclaims as he points over to Camilla and Lucius.

***

Felicia glances over, noticing Lucius and Camilla chatting about something. "Yes. I noticed that, Master," says Felicia as she is watching very closely at the fighters down below.

The two gladiators are so tired, but they kept up their fight as the crowd screams, urging them on. The Thraces catches the Hoplomachi in the side with his sword that tore into his skin as the blood dripped down his armor and onto the sand. The Hoplomachi takes his shield and smacks his opponent in the head with it. It does not faze him as the Thraeces flings his sword as he cuts deep, thin cuts into him, grabbing hold of his opponent and picking him up over his head and tossing him into the air like he was nothing. The Emperor sits up as he applauds and laughs. The Hoplomachi notices his spear from the beginning of the match. He quickly scrambles to his feet with the Thraeces quickly behind him. The Hoplomachi reaches out to grab his spear. The Thraeces steps on the Hoplomachi hand, crushing it under his foot. He takes his shield, hitting the Hoplomachi in the face; his mouth and nose bleed fiercely as his eyes begin to swell. Before too long, the Hoplomachi cannot see and the helmet feels like his head is being crushed.

The crowd chants, "Kill him, kill him!!" over and over. Cato looks on as he sees the very intense scene and then looks over at the Emperor for his reactions.

The Thraeces grabs his opponent, shaking him around roughly and then ripping his helmet off for the crowd to see the Hoplomachi face. The Thraeces then glances up to the Emperor as he awaits for a signal. The Emperor stands, hearing the crowd. Sticking up his hand and giving a large smile to the crowd, he motions a thumbs down! The Thraeces picks up the spear that had been chucked at him earlier in the fight and watches his opponent bow his head as he awaits his death. He cannot wait to see his loved ones in the afterlife.

The Thraeces stabs his opponent in the back of the neck with the spear, shoving as hard as he can until it makes a horrid crunching sound and the spear sticks out of the Hoplomachi throat. The people cheer loudly as the Thraeces stands in the middle of the arena, hearing the people cheer for him. Felicia stands on the tips of her toes, leaning far over the awning to get a better look of the winner. The Thraeces finally removes his helmet, revealing his face. Felicia is so anxious, but she cannot see his face just yet and can only see the back of his head. The winner waves in a circle as he slowly makes his way around.

Felicia notices his face and her jaw drops. She squeals with excitement! She noticed his face was tan as leather with a thick jaw line, sandy brown hair, and a medium build and chiseled chest. Felicia can't believe it! This warrior looks just like Radix! She shrieks with delight, jumping around.

She glances at Master Cato and says, "Master Cato! That is Radix! I cannot believe it!"

Cato looks at Felicia and sees her filled with much excitement. Cato has never seen Felicia smile that big before. It warms his heart seeing this. Now he questioned how, if possible, could Felicia and Radix be alone to talk.

Cato and Felicia wait for their area to clear out so they can leave. Calli is still very ill and is being carried in Cato's arms. Many people look at him oddly as he carries a slave, but he does not care. He knows it would not help any of them if Calli did not get well. They make their way to Lucius and Camilla's villa. Cato knows that Lucius and Camilla will not mind him putting his slave in his guest area for the time being. He looks at Felicia and asks her to please look over Calli while he finds Lucius to explain what has happened. Felicia walks to the kitchen area, grabbing a bowl of water and making her way back to the room. She rips a piece of fabric from an old dress she found in her bag. She wets it and places it over Calli's head. Felicia opens the wooden shutters, feeling the winds blow through and in a circle. She is hoping that will help Calli feel better.

Cato walks through the busy streets, finding Camilla looking at the jewelry. She holds the long chain that is decorated with green and red shiny jewels up to her chest then sees a matching ring. She laughs and says, "Oh, I have to buy these! They will be perfect for tonight's celebration!"

Lucius looks over to his wife. "That is fine but those jewels do not give you justice. They will only enhance your beauty!" Then, seeing Cato, he says, "Have you ever seen an oddly shaped fruit? They call it a mango? Where are your slaves, Cato?"

Cato picks up the mango and pays the vendor. "Yes, the mangos are delicious. Calli and Felicia purchased me some the last time they were at market. You need to try them; you will not be sorry. But I do need to speak to you regarding my slaves."

Lucius looks down at the oddly looking fruit and pays for two of them, taking a large bite out of one of the mangos before saying, "Ok, these are very refreshing and your slaves are very thoughtful to think of what type of food you may enjoy. But, go ahead, why do you need to speak to me about your slaves?"

Cato looks at his friend nervously. "Calli is very ill and I am hoping she can stay in my room tonight. And I am hoping that Felicia can stay with me as well to look after Calli. Do you think Camilla will have a problem with this? I do know you have quite a few healers in the city, but I was given stuff by my healer that should help her get well quickly. Though, I would feel better if Calli and Felicia both stayed with me tonight."

Lucius shakes his head and glares at Cato. "I do hope that your slave heals quickly and I see no problem with Felicia staying with you as well. It could help Calli heal faster knowing that Felicia is there caring for her. But if you need assistance throughout the night, please do not hesitate to let one of my slaves know and I will inform Camilla of what has happened."

Cato makes his way back to his room in the villa. He prays that Calli will be better by that night's celebration. Cato walks on and sees a small bouquet of flowers growing in a mass on the small hill next to the villa. He stops and grabs a few. The colors are very vibrant reds, oranges, yellows, and blues, and the scent is light enough that it will not over power the scenes making Calli feel more nauseous. He gathers them in a wet piece of fabric, hoping they make her feel better.

Cato walks in his room and sees Felicia sitting in a chair next to her, holding Calli's hand. She has lit a candle that is on the little table and it lets off a small glow. Cato walks over to the bed and sees a vase that is half filled with wine. He picks it up and dumps it out of the window then tells Felicia to go rinse it out and fill it with water. While she is away, Cato kneels down next to the bed and whispers a prayer for Calli to heal quickly, and then stands up and kisses her a top her head.

Felicia has the heavy vase of water and is being escorted back by Lucius. When they both walk in to see Cato's actions, Lucius raises an eyebrow. "Are we interrupting something, Cato?" he asks

Cato stands up, clearing his throat and ordering that Felicia sit the vase beside the bed, and then he places the flowers inside of it and walks out with Lucius following him.

Lucius is in shock to see his friend act that way and he raises his voice to him. "What the fucking hell was that? Are you falling in love with your slave?"

"Now hold on just a minute! Just because I kiss her head and bring her flowers does not mean I am falling in love with her. I have been told that flowers can make a sick person feel better. Besides, I am hoping I will not have to have a healer come in that will be more coin I will have to pay out. And Felicia will have to work even harder."

Lucius chuckles and replies, "Ok, my friend. You have never acted this way about a slave, but I do see your point. When one person gets ill, it does make it hard on everyone else. So I will pray that she does heal by tonight. Now, let's start this fucking party before the guests riot. I am sure my slaves can handle it while Felicia looks after Calli. Let's just get everything ready and if there is any change I am sure you will be informed. I have to get back to the market before Camilla spends all of the coin that I just won!"

***

Felicia places the dampened rag across Calli's head and rubs the ginger water across the seams of her lips.

"Wh- what happened? How did I get in here?" Calli questions as she begins to awaken.

Felicia grabs Calli's hand. "Shhh... Rest now, little sister. You got sick at the games and Master Cato took care of you, giving you a ginger rooted water and crackled bread. He then carried you back here to Sir Lucius and Mistress Camilla's villa. I have been looking after you since."

Calli looks around and sees the lit candle on the table and the bundle of flowers that sit in the vase. "Where did these come from?" she questions.

Felicia's eyes widen as she answers. "Well, Master Cato brought them to you. He was hoping that the bright colors would help make you feel better. And look, it did just that!"

Calli's eyes widen as she sits up completely in the bed and says, "Let me get this straight. Master Cato carried me all the way here from the Amphitheater and he also brought me these flowers? Oh my goodness! I am speechless, Felicia."

Cato takes his time walking back to his room. He looks across the hill at the sun that was going down. The sunset was a breathtaking color of orange and pink. He sees that the sky is a light purple color as he walks up to his door and feels the breeze blow in and the pollen that fills the entry way of his room. Then the sounds of Calli and Felicia talking catches his ear. He quickly throws the doors open to see Calli beginning to sit up. He can tell that she was still groggy, but her strength was returning to her and each minute that passed she was feeling better!

Chapter 9

Calli grows quiet when she sees Cato standing inside the entry way of the door. Felicia turns to Cato to see the excitement in his eyes to know that Calli will be fine. She still insists that she help out at the celebration. Cato is unsure about this, but he knows he can trust Calli. He exits the room and tells both Felicia and Calli to take their time, but not to be too late making it to the celebration that starts in just a few hours. Calli and Felicia get ready for the party by brushing each other's hair and then tying it up off of their shoulders. They each pick up a flower and rub it across their wrists. The smell from the few petals of those flowers are divine and make them both feel pretty for their master. Felicia tells Calli about that day's last match, and seeing that the Thraces was Radix, and how surprised and thrilled that she was to see his face. Calli is happy for her friend and hopes that Radix will remember his once lovely slave that served him.

The gladiators are led to the streets as the large crowd cheers, wishing to see a glimpse or to touch their favorite fighter. Lucius and Camilla push their way through the mob of fans. Camilla bumps into a horde of women who are grabbing at the fighters. Camilla lightly traces her hand over Radix's rough fingers. He stops, glancing over at her. He cannot help noticing a look that she gives him. He glares at her while Camilla smiles softly at the winner. Lucius is in a wonderful mood and has a large smile on his face. He grabs his wife's waist and clenches her hand then walks her back to their home. Lucius looks behind them, seeing the large crowd of people following them back to their villa. Their home will be very busy.

Cato, Calli, and Felicia make their way to Lucius and Camilla's home. They walk in and notice all the people already there. Cato looks at his two slaves and he sees the color has returned to Calli's face and she is feeling better than earlier. Calli and Felicia are aware that they are to serve the food and wine to Cato and the other guests. Calli and Felicia start off washing Cato's hands. Then one hands him a piece of boar meat, bread, and wine.

Calli and Felicia stand by, watching as the other people get their hands washed by the other slaves. Calli thinks back on what Felicia said about Radix and she has a great idea on how to get her and Radix in the same area to meet. Calli knows that it will be dangerous, but she knows it will work. Calli walks around the area, noticing all the slaves that are fanning the other guests or giving massages. She makes her way upstairs quietly then finds a room that is empty with no people in it.

Calli looks around the room and notices the different masks that are hanging on the wall. They are all decorated with different jewels with each one having a different shape for the eyes and the nose. These masks are used if a royal wants to have an anonymous affair with a gladiator and not have anyone find out. What happens then is the royal and the gladiator would meet in a designated bedroom, both wearing the matching mask that would hide their faces.

Calli is so thrilled and knows exactly what she will do. She silently creeps across the floor, trying to not disturb anything. She sees a set of white pearls sitting on a table. They are so pretty and elegant. She picks them up and places them across her chest, looking at herself into the mirror and noticing they have a slight sent of a powder. Next to the necklace is a jar full of white and blue feathers. The feathers tickle Calli's nose.

This room alone is breathtaking. It is a dark pink color with a gold color bordering around the ceiling. The window opens up to the view of the ocean and the sounds of the waves crashing into the rocks. There is a large picture of Camilla hanging above the bed. Calli looks closely at this picture. She realizes that Felicia and Camilla are the same shape, height, and hair color and even their eyes are the about the same color.

Calli quickly grabs a set of masks, two white feathers, and the pearls that sat on the table. She looks around the room and takes a deep breath.

"Here we go! This has to work!" she says to herself, reaching for the door and sneaking out quietly and back down the hallway to the room that she and Felicia were sharing with Master Cato. She looks under the bed and sees her bag, dragging it out and placing the mask inside of it along with the feathers and the pearls. She is so nervous. She turns around to see the pearls had fallen out of the bag that she tossed underneath the bed. She shoves the necklace back in and leaves the bag across the couch and walks back to the door.

Just as she is to leave the room, Fuscus walks in and is surprised to see Calli standing there.

"OH! Sir Fuscus! You startled me!" Calli exclaimed.

Fuscus looks around the room, noticing her standing there in surprise. "Calli, what are you doing?"

Calli thinks quickly as she blurts out, "Oh, when did you arrive, Sir Fuscus? I was looking for more wine! I thought we had some in here. Master really enjoyed the one that was in this vase, but there was only water in here."

Fuscus glances at her. "I have been here for some time. I was just visiting with everyone. Cato told me that you were ill. I am glad that you are feeling better. And the wine is in the other room, Calli…with the food; where you should be. If Lucius or Camilla catch you wondering around their house, you will get whipped and Cato will not be able to help you."

Calli hurries out of the room, heading back to Felicia. She returns just in time for the next course. Calli grabs the small bowl and begins washing the guests' hands and fingers, drying them with a soft cloth. After she finishes washing everyone's hands, she decides to sneak her way out of the upper house to the lower part and making her way to the ludus through a secret entry. Calli hopes that she does not get caught by the guards.

***

Felicia has got to get out of there for just a few minutes. The sounds and commotion are giving her a headache. Walking out on the small balcony, she stares up at the stars. It is such a beautiful night out and the moon is perfect with not a cloud in sight. She looks down across the grass and sees Calli cut across the small grassy knoll and knows that she is up to something. She knows that she cannot follow her, but she will question her when she returns.

187

***

Calli looks both ways, making it past the small door, and rushes through the confusing corridors. She is so nervous and fears of being caught make her even more nervous. She is thinking of what she would say if she did get caught before she whispers, "Radix? Radix, where are you?" There are four guards talking when they see Calli walking through the very confusing floors.

All four of them look at her oddly and ask, "Hey you! Slave, what are you doing down here?"

Calli nervously stammers and says, "Domina sent me. Domina is asking for me to send him a message and she sent me to tell him." They look at her with no questions asked, taking her to the cell where Radix was.

Calli quietly whispers, "Radix? Radix are you in there?"

The man on the other side of the door answers in a raspy voice, "Who are you, and what do you want?"

"You do not know me? My name is Calli. I am slave to Master Cato, and serve The House of Felix. My sister is..."

188

Before Calli can finish, the man on the opposite side says, "Yes. My brother told me that your Master asked of me. I do not know who your Dominus is. Do you know how long it has taken me to get the trust of my Master? If your Master was to know that you are down in the gladiator cells, I am sure he would not be happy. So whatever you are here for, you are wasting your time."

"Are you Radix? That is all I want to know." The man glances through the bars where Calli stares her dark, green emerald eyes at him.

The man sighs. "Yes, I am Radix. But, I do not know of your sister. I have not had slaves for a very long time."

"I have risked a lot coming here to speak to you. I am only doing this because I love my sister. I have a plan, but you have to trust me. Can you do this for me, Radix?"

"I do not even know you, and you ask me to trust you? Look, woman, if I am caught trying to defy or shame my owners I will be beaten and then sold! Do you really think I will risk all of what I have finally earned for you or your sister?

You must be insane!" Radix exclaims.

"I do not want to get you in trouble with your Domina or Dominus."

Radix lets out a big sigh. "I must be insane, but, yes, I can trust you."

Calli turns to go and says, "I will send my friend, Sir Fuscus, to give you more instructions. Just know that your Domina will be sending for you soon."

***

Calli realizes she needs to hurry and get back to the party before anyone notices her missing. She rushes through the corridors, up the rickety old wooden stairs making it back to the celebrations in time as a group of people walk out. She rushes up the stairs, making her way inside. She notices Fuscus sitting talking to a slave. Not wanting to interrupt them, she stands by Master Cato.

The night goes on as planned. Everyone is drinking and enjoying themselves. Calli walks through the house, looking around as she tries to work her way around the house. The house is big. It has a main bedroom, four guest bedrooms, Slave quarters that slept many, and even a bathhouse! It is decorated with several paintings, fruit trees, and flowers that grow around and upward toward the ceiling. If it wasn't for the ludus in the back, you would never know.

Calli notices there is a very large, empty bedroom way in the very back. It has a balcony that looks over the river that flows below. The bed is in the center of the room, and it is very large. There are many different color sheets that go across the ceiling as they drape over the bed. The walls are colored in a light blue, with the smell of refreshing lavender wafting through the air. There are numerous candles that are mounted on one of the walls. Pictures of Aphrodite, Eros, and Peitho are painted on the adjoining walls. Calli rushes into the room that she and Felicia are sharing with Master Cato. She sees Fuscus and informs him of the plan. "Are you fucking insane? Calli, we could die if we get caught!" he says.

"No, I am not. Please, tell Cato that I am still not feeling well and that I need to get some sleep."

Fuscus walks back to the party and tells Cato. "Calli is not feeling well. She went to lie down."

Cato looks over at Felicia, asking her to go check on Calli.

Felicia knew something was going on so she quickly walks into the room where Calli is laying down. "What is going on, Calli? I know you are not sick! And I am not stupid. I know you are up to something!"

Calli sits up and stares at Felicia through the flame. She can see that she is very upset. She finally breaks the silence and says, "Okay, okay, I will tell you. No; I will show you." Reaching under the bed, she pulls the bag out and carefully removes the items.

Felicia sees all of the beautiful things lying across the bed. "Where did you get all of that? Did you steal those from Domina Camilla?"

"No, I did not steal them! I am borrowing them and I will return all of them when everything is finished."

Felicia looks puzzled. "What do you mean when everything is finished? Calli! What are you up to?"

"Nothing; just planning on a way for you and Radix to get together. Look, it is a really easy plan. I notice that you and Camilla look very much alike, if you are wearing this." Calli holds up a mask.

Felicia hisses at Calli. "No, goodness no! That plan will never work, Calli. I do not look like a royal."

Calli chuckles at her and says, "That is why I have the pearls and the feathers. You will look like her and when the guards bring Radix up after they put him in the room, you walk out and do not say a word. They will not think anything about it."

Felicia still stands there staring at Calli and shrieks. "I think that the heat today has made you mad! And I think it's a crazy plan, but I would love to see Radix again. Gosh, I do not know, Calli!"

Calli giggles at Felicia and says, "You worry too much. Just trust me. This will work."

Felicia nervously agrees and keeps it quiet. She said one last thing before leaving the room. "I worry that if we are caught that Master Cato will punish us so severely or sell us. I could not live having to serve the rest of my life working in the mines or for another Master. But, Calli, I will trust you because you are my best friend and my sister."

***

Fuscus has finally decided to go ahead and help Calli with her plan. He walks down the stairs and through the corridor to the holding cell, looking for the guards, but instead he gets turned around and runs into the teacher who is making his rounds. Fuscus does not say much; only a simple message. "Domina has summoned Radix tomorrow, and he is to be wearing this." Fuscus hands the teacher the grayish blue mask.

The teacher chuckles and says, "Of course. We will make sure he is ready."

Fuscus then makes his way back to the main house and slips into his guest room to go to sleep. When Fuscus walks in and notices a red headed slave awaiting him, he stands at the entrance and leans against the wall. He is very surprised to come back to his room to this. He questions the lady about who she is. She giggles, removing her clothing and slowly tracing her hands across her bare breasts while her tongue is tracing over her lips.

"I am Jade. I was sent by my Domina and Dominus to please you for the night. Do I not entice your wants and needs, sir?"

"Yes. Oh, yes, you do," says Fuscus, smiling and closing the door behind him.

Jade stands up, kicking her dress to the floor. She leans in, kissing Fuscus as she begins running her hands across his chest and down his torso. He grabs her waist, pulling her to and then nuzzling his face into her breast, kissing and licking around her perky nipples and reaching up to grab her hair and force her head back. She lets out a low moan, feeling his teeth graze her neck. She reaches inward, beginning to grope his growing, erected cock and working her hands up and down slowly in a small circular motion. Fuscus bites down on her neck, pushing her face down on the small bed. He grits his teeth and growling low in her ear while ordering her to not move. Jade lifts her head, glancing over her shoulder to see Fuscus with a want in his eyes that she has never seen before from another man. Jade gives him a little grin then traces her tongue across her lips, shifting around and pressing her round plump ass against his hardened cock. Teasing him a good while and tracing her fingers across it, she inhales deeply, letting out a low moan while she enjoys the feeling of it throb against her skin. He lifts his hand up, swatting as hard as he can against her bare skin. She jerks from the stinging sensation, popping out in a sweat. Fuscus presses his hands against her bare ass, pulling her ass cheeks apart and then forcing his cock deep inside her very wet pussy while reaching up with his other hand and grasping her hair. With a hard yank of her head, he pulls her back onto him.

She grinds her soaking pussy into him, feeling as her movements against him cause Fuscus to moan loudly when she moves back and forth, teasing him by lifting up as he feels himself almost slip out of her, making him ram his throbbing cock deep inside her and then grabbing her hips and pounding her as hard as he can. Jade throws her head back, sitting up against him. Jade reaches back, grasping his hair and giving it a good tug with the other hand while grabbing her breasts and running her hand down her body to place her fingers over her moist, and now enlarged, clit barely, touching it and its very sensitive area. Fuscus makes a growling noise like that of a wolf, gritting his teeth and jerking her head back to lean in give Jade a long, hard kiss, almost losing it when he hears Jade let out a low whimper in between the kisses. She bites her lip as she feels him pounding her with such force. Stopping for a brief moment and flipping her to her back, he takes her legs and pulls them far apart; his nails dig into her inner thighs. She lets out a hissing sound.

Jade reaches up and claws at his chest, the stinging sensation of her nails tearing at his chest and leaving small, but deep scratches that feel like small swords slicing at his flesh. She sits up, slowly rocking her hips side to side and begging for more while wrapping her legs tightly around him.

The feeling of his nails digging deep into her flesh followed with him biting down hard on her shoulders like a lion tearing at its food sends her over the edge with her body

196

shaking and convulsing. Fuscus lets out a long and deafening moan just as he releases himself inside of her. The lovers both fall over, panting heavily and shortly after falling sound asleep.

A little while later, the slave leaves Fuscus' room and makes her way back to the kitchen area and the slave quarters.

Later that day, Cato, Fuscus, Calli, and Felicia walk around the city and begin exploring the vendors. After which, they make their way back to Lucius and Camilla's. As they are walking in, they are led to the back area where the gladiators are training. They all stand at the balcony, watching as they see the men fighting and practicing their moves. The sands glisten against the sun and the wind picks up, sending the scent of sweat and blood swirling around the villa.

The teacher shouts at them. "Do any of you actually think that your Dominus will give you a wooden sword and make you a free man?!" The man scoffs "You all remember this; he has a contract to keep! You all pledged to be trained and live by our rules, and that is where I come in. Your Master makes sure that he feeds you, gives you shelter, and clothing! But for all this to happen you must make him coin! Do you all understand?!"

All the men shout, "YES!"

Fuscus and Cato watch as the fighters practice their moves before they fight each other. Lucius and Camilla come out and invite them to go into the city with them to see the bundles of new slaves that came. Cato agrees to go, but says he would like for Calli and Felicia to go to the bathing house. Camilla kindly offers them to use theirs. Calli and Felicia go to the bathing area. Felicia is washed and scented oil is rubbed into her body. As they leave the bathing room and head back to the guest room, the sun was just dipping under the hills as they made it back from the auction house.

The party for that night has already begun and there were voices throughout the villa. Calli hugs her sister, giving her reassurance that the outcome will work out and there is nothing to worry about. Their friend, Fuscus, waits in the hall as he paces back and forth nervously. The guards lead Radix to the villa and the female slaves ready him for the night as they rub silver paint all over his body then place the mask over his head to conceal him.

In the room across the way, Calli readies Felicia as she brushes her hair, pulling it back away from her face and then grabbing a few strands as it falls in little ringlets around her face. Felicia picks up a small bottle of lightly fragranced oil that smells of lavender. She rubs the oil across her wrists, behind her ears, and creases of her calves. Calli wraps a soft, sheer fabric around Felicia's chest in an X, crisscrossed around her upper region to just above her navel. Calli then grabs the eye paints out of her bag and traces the light blue over her sister's eyes. She walks to the small window, plucking a pomegranate off the tree and busting it open to the small seeds. Calli rubs the seeds across Felicia's lips until they were the perfect color red.

To break the silence, Calli says, "Felicia, stop! Don't worry so much. This is the only thing I could think to do for you and Radix to meet again. And like I said, Camilla and you are the same height, hair color …well, everything. Also, here—" She hands the mask and pearls to Felicia, who looks at it as she traces her hands over it, noticing the small pearls that glisten.

"Calli, I am so scared! If Radix finds out or if Camilla catches on! Oh, Calli, I am so very nervous. Also, if Master Cato finds out he will be so hurt and mad!"

Fuscus taps on the door as the guards walk past with Radix. Calli jumps and hurries to get the door, seeing Fuscus on the other side and nodding her head to let Fuscus know that she understands. Fuscus turns and makes his way down the stairs to the celebration. Felicia takes in a deep breath, and then slides the mask over her face.

She turns to Calli and asks, "How does it look?"

Calli turns to her, placing the pearls over Felicia's face and the few feathers in her hair. "Perfect!"

The two walk out of the room, going their separate ways. Felicia walks past the guards. They never suspect anything, thinking that she is Camilla. Felicia walks through the door and stands by the bed. A cool breeze blows through the room. Radix runs his hands through his hair as he catches the scent of lavender in the air. He turns around to see the gorgeous lady standing before him. He doesn't say a word as he walks over to her and traces his hands across her body.

***

Radix then whispers, "With each touching feel of you, my cock grows, Domina" as he turns her toward him, picking her up and cradling her in his arms then dropping her to the bed.

She arches her back as he climbs on top of her. Felicia gives him a warm smile, tracing her fingertips over his chiseled chest. Felicia moans low as his hardened cock finds it way inside of her wetness. The paint runs down his body as he slides his tongue down her cleavage. Felicia spins around quickly, pressing her back side to Radix. She groans loudly as he grabs her waist and pounds deeper inside of her. Radix lets out a deafening moan as he places his hands over her neck, squeezing just enough so Felicia feels a tingling feeling. She lets out a small gasp as she digs her nails into the fabric of the bed. Radix and Felicia fall back to the bed. They lay across the bed as the thunder claps and the lightning flashes in the distance. The clouds open up and the rain pours in the room as the winds rush in, blowing the candles out. Radix lets out a sigh as he stands up and wraps his cloth around his waist. He glances over as the lighting strikes, seeing the fabric across her body. It draping and falls just down her shoulders as she stands with her back facing him. Radix looks again as the thunder cracks like a whip in across the lands. He notices the marking on her shoulder and rushes quickly to Felicia's side as he notices what used to be his old marking over this lady's shoulder blade.

Radix stares in shock as he says, "Why do you wear my old marking? It has been so long that I have seen it, I have almost forgotten what it looks like. Do my eyes deceive me?" Felicia says nothing, trying to quickly make her way to the door. Radix rushes ahead of her, stopping her from exiting. He questions, "My dear sweet, Felicia, is it you? Is it true; have the Gods brought you to me once again?"

Felicia feels the tears fall from her face, trickling to the floor. She gasps for air, slowly removing her mask that had covered her face. She answers, "Yes, Radix, it is I." She reaches up and slowly takes off his mask as well.

Radix steps back in astonishment. "How could this be?"

Felicia walks toward him. "I am now serving in the House of Felix and my Master is Cato. I am under the protection of him."

Radix raises his voice. "This storm has worsened; we have angered the Gods! See the rains as it pours in. See they send flash of lightning down upon us! If my Domina finds out what just happened I will surely be beat, sold, or crucified."

Felicia speaks up. "No, Radix! Camilla will not find out. My sister, Calli, set this up. Even you thought I was Camilla."

"I do love you, Felicia, but we cannot be together. I must make coin for my Master until I am granted my freedom."

Radix and Felicia hug each other tightly and they feel like their hearts beat as one soul, though one half is missing.

The rains finally slow to a mere drizzle. The sun shines over the lands, and Radix and Felicia go their separate ways. Felicia creeps her way back to where Cato and Calli sleep. Radix is still in shock, but he slowly makes his way back to his cell where he finds it hard to sleep though he needs to be ready for that day's practice.

***

Fuscus, Cato, and Lucius watch from above as they see the gladiators practice for the games. The women are inside dressing for that day's events. They make their way back to the amphitheater. Cato notices Felicia eyeing a statue in the stall.

Cato calls out to her and asks, "Felicia, why do you keep looking at the same statue?"

Felicia looks to the ground as she says, "I like it, Master. I don't know why; it just always catches my eye."

Cato chuckles and says, "Ok, little one. Come along".

The very beginning of the games finally begin with the guards shuffling the convicts to the center of the arena and handing them rusted swords as they are being told to fight. The men chase each other as they hack and cut one another. The fans cheer and yell as the men dig their swords in each other as

203

a thin, scraggly haired man stands shaking in the arena as he jumps in the air and lands hard as he slashes another man's throat. The gates are raised again as a large black and orange striped tiger and a larger, black panther walk out. The smell of the blood on the scared men as they all stand petrified then run in different directions take off running for their life, some dropping their weapons, permeates the air. The tiger leaps on a man, digging his razor sharps claws into his back as he sinks his teeth into the man's skull. The panther teases his prey, backing two men back in a corner and then clawing both men and catching one in the middle of the face. The other man shakes and trembles in fear, knowing he will not make it out alive, and as soon as he takes off a man jumps from out of nowhere and plunges a spear deep into the man's abdomen.

Lucius, Camilla, and Fuscus clap with the crowd. Cato, Calli, and Felicia stare as the cougar and the tiger are lead back to their cages. Guards walk out to the arena and blow their trumpets loudly. Calli and Felicia anxiously await the final match as the two gladiators walk out.

Lucius leans over, kissing his wife gently on the cheek and showing a big smile at how happy and pleased he is as he is looking out to the enormous crowd of people that are cheering and chanting loudly. He stands, raising his hand in a waving motion and greets the crowd. "Now, the match that everyone has been waiting for,—Radix and Tascis!"

The crowd claps loudly when both men let out their warrior cries, running toward each other with their weapons in hand. Radix grips his shield and sword as the Tascis swings his heavy mallet in the air, smashing it to the ground. Calli moves closer to Cato, gripping his hand. Felicia gasps, watching the two men try to destroy the other. Lucius and Camilla watch as Radix slides under his opponent's legs, smashing his shield into Tascis' knee. Radix leaps up as he grabs a bit of sand and tosses it in his opponent's eyes, blinding him long enough as Radix brings his sword over his head, slicing the man's back wide open. Blood gushes down Tascis back as he throws his mallet, hitting Radix across his face. Tascis laughs as blood rushes out of Radix's mouth.

Camilla looks at Felicia's reaction to Radix being injured. Felicia hides her face as she hears the crowd of people scream. Tascis picks up Radix's shield, throwing it at Radix's chest. Radix bends over in pain as the edges of the shield enter his chest and slide down, making deep cuts. Tascis picks up his mallet, smashing it against Radix leg. Radix screams in pain before grabbing his sword and plunging it deep into Trascis' chest.

The amphitheater explodes in a loud roar when the crowd cheers, "Radix, Radix…!"

Felicia jumps to her feet as she cheers loudly and hugs Calli. Camilla and Lucius can't help but notice Felicia's reactions when Radix wins his match. Fuscus looks over, noticing Cato, Calli, and Felicia with them all beginning to exit the arena quickly. Lucius asks Fuscus if he would mind escorting Camilla back to the villa while he finishes up some business. Fuscus agrees, and he and Camilla leave.

Cato, Calli, and Felicia make it back to Lucius and Camilla's and they are all exhausted and cannot wait to head back home. They enjoyed it when they would visit Cato's friends, but they wanted to be able to sleep under their own roof.

Calli and Felicia fold all of their clothes, putting them all in a pile as the other places it in the small bag. They both speak lowly amongst themselves, as Calli says, "Felicia, I don't mean to be rude, but how did your time go with Radix last night?"

"Oh Calli! It was everything I had dreamt of," Felicia replies.

Calli smiles. "Well, he never found out it was you."

Felicia gives Calli a long stare and Calli looks deep into her friend's eyes. "Felicia, please tell me? Did Radix find out you were not Camilla?"

"Well, at the very end he did find out the truth," Felicia says, swallowing hard.

***

Camilla and Fuscus make it back to the villa. Camilla walks past the other guest rooms, over hearing Calli and Felicia's conversation. "Felicia, I don't want all the details of you and Radix from last night, but I can only imagine it was very romantic! And the best part is the guards had no idea it was you because of the mask you were wearing; they thought you were Camilla! I told you it would work and your secret is safe with me!"

Camilla is outraged as she overhears this secret! She storms into the rear bedroom where her masks are. She notices that two masks are missing. When Lucius returns, he finds Camilla in an uproar with tears flowing down her red face and yelling so loud it could possibly be heard in the afterlife.

Lucius screams, "What is the meaning of this madness you are going about having? Are you aware that you have all the slaves scared of you in fear that you may sell them at the market tomorrow, if they ask what is wrong?" She picks up a glass, throwing it to the wall and it shatters and falls to the floor. Again, Lucius demands to know what has made her so enraged.

Camilla throws her glass of wine, jumping up and down like a child, and screams, "That little whore of Cato's slept with Radix! Can you believe it?!"

Lucius looks at his wife in surprise and says, "I do not see what the big fuss is about? He is a slave, she is a slave."

Camilla glares at her husband, giving him a very mean, evil look and demanding that he tell Cato. Lucius knows if he does not do this he will never hear the end of it from Camilla. So he orders that his guards go search and find Cato, Fuscus, Calli, and Felicia and bring them back to Lucius' villa immediately. The guards saddle their horses and ride off into the city, trying to catch up to the four.

***

The guards ride up just as Cato and the rest are about to leave the city and say, "Apologies, Sir Cato, but we are here to inform you and the rest of your party that Lucius wishes to speak to all of you and it is urgent!"

The four look at each other, turning back and returning to the villa. They are all waiting to hear what the urgency is and why Lucius had them all return. Lucius and Camilla walk into the entry way and they both have a very ill look on their face.

Cato asks, "Lucius, what has happened that you had to summon us all back to your doorstep?"

Lucius puts his glass of wine down hard on the table. He begins pointing and shaking his finger at Cato and yells, "I think you should know, that last night while we were all enjoying the celebration, apparently your slaves went behind our backs and helped themselves by plotting to sleep with Radix; and if that wasn't enough, your two slaves stole two masks that have been in my family for many years."

Camilla, still red in the face, stomps over and points her finger at Calli and Felicia. "She is a little whore, and this one is a little manipulator and very sneaky. I cannot believe you trust them!"

Cato stares at his friend in disbelief, standing in shock as he says, "Lucius, my apologies, but are you sure?" Cato glances over at Calli and Felicia then looks over at Fuscus and says, "Tell me this is not the truth that comes from his mouth!"

Calli and Felicia feel the walls caving in on them as they both begin to tremble with fear but do not cry.

Cato feels himself about to lose his temper while hearing the accusations that everyone is saying about Calli and Felicia. He quickly stands by them and yells, "Kneel!"

Camilla, still furious, screams at the guards and demanding they bring Radix to them at once. Both of the guards reply, "Yes, Domina."

***

Radix stands up straight, staring to the wall and not saying a word. His nerves are palpable.

Lucius walks over to Radix and says in a demanding voice, "Radix, did you lay with Dominus Cato's slave, Felicia?"

Radix looks at his Master and replies, "Dominus, yes I did. But, I did not know until later that is was her."

Camilla walks over and asks the guards and Radix, "Did you see a mask on the slave girl, Felicia?"

Radix and the guards all answer, "Yes, Domina, but, I thought it was you."

Camilla gawks with an evil laugh leaving her lips. "ME?! Why would you think she was me? Do I look like her? Tell me, do I look like a slave? Do I smell like a slave? How dare you insult me? I should have you all sold to the mines!" she says as she turns her back and glares at everyone in the room.

Radix looks around then answers nervously, "Many apologies, Domina. I was told by the teacher and the guards that you summoned me and insisted that I wear the mask that was given to me."

Camilla screams for the teacher and the guards from the other night. The men come rushing in, bowing before Camilla and Lucius.

Camilla glares at the guards in such hatred and rage that she cannot even get the words to leave her mouth. "Lucius, I am leaving this situation for you to handle!" She stomps away more furious and the slaves around take cover as they hear her loud footsteps clacking against the stoned floor then the loud bang of the door closing behind her with the deafening, raged high pitch scream.

Lucius looks around the room, noticing everyone staring at him, and then runs his hands through his hair

211

followed by wiping his face with his sleeve and looking to the ceiling. "Ok! Fine; fucking shit! Did someone come to you and say that your Domina was summoning Radix?"

The guards stammer and say in fear, "Dominus, one of Cato's slaves came to the cells and demanded to see Radix. Your friend, Sir Fuscus, came as well."

Lucius' jaw drops. "Why did Fuscus come to the cells?"

"He said that we needed to bring Radix to Domina the following night and we did. Later that night, the person we thought was Domina walked right past us."

Lucius glares to the teacher. "What did Fuscus say to you? And you better answer quickly or you will be whipped!" he shouts.

The teacher replies, "He said, that Domina wanted Radix to wear a mask and then handed me the mask before quickly departing."

Fuscus eases his way through. "Yes; yes, Lucius, this is true. I did do this. I will not lie. Though, I did not think it was a good idea, Calli said that it would work."

Lucius' mouth drops as he chuckles then repeats in an arrogant voice, "You did not think it was a good idea, but Calli said it would work? Tell me, do you always take stupid, idiotic ideas from a slave?"

"Not always, but she is my friend," he says with his chest stuck out and chin high.

Cato stands, looking at them in shock and hearing the guards and the teacher tell of how Calli and Fuscus planned to get Radix and Felicia together. Camilla storms back in, pushing her husband and the guards out of her way.

"Move out of my way!" Camilla screams, standing in front of Felicia and Calli. She glares down at the two slaves kneeling at their Master's feet. Camilla then shouts in their ears, "If you were my slaves, I would have you whipped until there was no skin on your back then crucified for lying and thievery! I don't know what your Master plans on your punishment being, but I do hope it is severe!"

Cato sees Calli and Felicia shutter in fear so he interrupts Camilla. "Many apologies, Camilla. No worries; I will punish them, but you are correct to say they are not your slaves and they are *mine*. I will handle their punishments and not you. But I honestly do not believe they stole your masks;

they have to be here." Cato looks at Calli and Felicia, who weep with fear then over at Fuscus, who stands with his back to the wall with a look of disgust on his face, then over to Lucius, who was so mad he was turning red and had veins popping out of his forehead. Cato runs his fingers through Felicia's hair as he leans down and asks her in a calming tone, "Felicia, where did you place the masks when you left the room?"

Felicia cries out. "I could have sworn that I hung them up. It was before I returned to the guest room that we were sleeping in. I wore the mask back in the room then waited as the guards took Radix back to the cell. Master, I promise you I did not steal anything!"

Cato clears his throat. "Little One, are you sure you had two masks in your possession, or just the one when you returned to the room?" he asked.

Felicia looks up with red, swollen eyes. "It was both of them."

Camilla looks at Radix, and then yells at the guards. "Take him back to his cell. Lucius will speak to him later."

Lucius clears his throat. He is still very upset at the situation he is now in. "Cato," he begins, "I am sorry to disrespect, but you, my friend, are too nice on your slaves. Now look at what has happened! If you would not be so lenient and nice to them this would not have happened!"

Camilla calls on their slaves to check all the rooms and demands that the guards check the bags that their guests had brought. All the slaves are made to search everywhere for the missing masks. They find the one that Felicia had worn behind a curtain, but the one that Radix had used was nowhere to be found. The longer they look and the item not be retrieved, the more pissed Camilla got. The guards are then informed to look in the bags of Fuscus, Cato, Calli, and Felicia. The guards take everything and toss it to the floor. Again, No mask. They dump the bag that Fuscus came with, rummaging through his clothes. They find a silver goblet, and in a lightly tied white sheet was the gray mask.

Everyone stares in shock with the story flying around the villa just as quickly as they had dumped out the belongings.

Fuscus' mouth drops as he stands there stunned in disbelief and shaking his head, saying over and over again, "No, it was not me! Lucius, Camilla, we have known each other for many years and I have never stolen from you then. Why would I steal from you now?!"

Lucius drops his head, feeling betrayed and calling for his guards. "Take this thief to a fucking holding cell! Get him out of my face before I order his death!"

Cato says, "Fuscus? But this does not make sense. Why would he do this?"

Camilla chuckles and says, "Because he is greedy; a thief and a liar!"

"He is none of those," Cato replies. "Camilla, you know that those words that leave your mouth are not true! He would do anything for you and your husband!"

"Yes, it is true. You are too blind to see it, Cato! Do you not see what your so called friend did to my husband?" Camilla shouts, turning around and leaving the room and any more discussion. She looks at three slaves that are now cleaning up a mess from a broken vase and yells at them. "Get me some wine!" The slaves hurry out of their Domina's view, rushing to the cellar to fetch what she has asked for.

***

Lucius stands outside the cell where Radix sleeps, playing the twist of events in his head. Without a second thought, he marches in and looks at Radix. "Just so you are

216

aware, if you win and succeed the next two fights I will grant you your freedom. If you lose, then you will remain in my ludus. Until you die!"

Radix sits on his bed and then speaks up. "I understand, Dominus."

"We will see, Radix," Lucius says as he is turning to leave the cell. Lucius returns to the villa, more enraged and pissed than before. "I will not be made to look like a fool in my own house! Fuscus will be executed in two days," he declares while looking over at Cato.

Cato and Lucius walk out as Lucius screams at the top of his lungs. "Damn it, what the fucking shit is going on? I haven't a clue about the goings on in my own house! Thievery lies, and who knows what else!"

Cato stares down at the land below and says, "Lucius, my friend, we go back a long ways. We played together as kids and were taught by the same person. Our fathers fought beside each other during times of battle. I will find out why Fuscus stole your property and why Calli and Felicia pulled their little stunt. Before arriving here, I was looking for papers on Radix; Felicia asked me if I could find out any information on him."

217

"Are you even mad that your slave lied to you and lay with Radix?"

"That is hard to answer. She has not been under my protection that long. Plus, I did not pay coin for her. She is only under my protection because she used to be Anton's slave and she saved my life."

Lucius nods his head. "I understand that, but she has brought shame on your name. She is still under your care and resides in the House of Felix. So I would like to know what you plan to do!"

"I am aware of all of this. I offer my apologies. No need to worry; I will find out the truth."

***

Camilla throws herself on the bed in a fit of rage as she stares at the ceiling and then rolls over and asks her slave, "Do you think I am crazed for being furious that one of Cato's slaves lay with Radix?"

Her slave glances up with the look of fear across her face. "No, Domina; of course not. But if I may say…" The slave goes silent, afraid to finish.

"Well? Speak!"

The slave goes on, "Do you think Fuscus put her up to it?"

Camilla busts up laughing. "Well, he would be given enough time to steal the masks?" She continues to laugh, but then sobers up to bark and order at the slave. "Bring me more wine."

As the slave heads down to the cellar, Felicia and Calli stay kneeling and not saying a word to each other. Camilla stomps around, throwing items as she tantrums back and forth, up and down the hall way. If it could be thrown and broken, it most certainly was. All anyone could hear was the sound of glass breaking in the background. It sounded like a war was going on in the villa.

***

Calli and Felicia kneel next to one another, whispering back and forth. "I know I put those masks back, Calli. I just know I did!"

"Do you think that someone planted those masks in Sir Fuscus bag?" Calli asks in response. "Whoever did this must really hate Sir Fuscus, and us as well."

Felicia glances over at Calli and nods her agreement. "I do not wish to point fingers and accuse anyone, Calli. But I feel awful!"

Cato and Lucius walk back in and see the slaves bowing their heads and staring at the floor. "What exactly where you two thinking? Did you not think I would find out?" Cato asks. Calli goes to stand up, but Cato stops her with a shout. "What are you doing? I did not say to stand up. Stay exactly how you are! Now, I said, tell me what you and Felicia were thinking?" Calli bows her head as she stares at the floor. "WELL?" Cato continues, his voice louder and deeper than they'd ever heard. Calli had to admit that she was a little bit scared of this man who had been nothing but kind to her in the past. "I only wanted to see my friend happy, Master. That is all I wanted. I did ask Fuscus to help me, but that was to just tell me when the guards brought him to the room." Felicia glares at the floor with her hands behind her back.

Lucius walks in and interrupts Cato as he says, "Sounds to me like they need to be reminded of who is in charge! Would you care for my whip, Cato?"

Cato shakes his head as he walks over to Felicia. "What did you think would come of this after you lay with Radix? Did you think he would be allowed to marry you?"

220

"I did not know," Felicia answers. "No; I did not think that, Master, but I cannot lie and say I do not love Radix." Cato shakes his head as he walks away in disbelief.

***

Lucius chuckles as he sees Fuscus being beaten so bad he can barely stand as he grabs to the chains that hold his battered body. He has two black eyes, a broken nose, bloodied mouth, and bruises covering all sides of his body.

Lucius says, "Did you not think you would get caught? You fucking fool! You do not steal from my home and get away with it! You will pay dearly for ever betraying me!"

Fuscus looks up at him and says in a pain filled tone, "Lucius, I swear to the Gods I do not know how the items came in my possession. I swear on my life. You have to believe me. All I did that night was go to my room where one of your slave girls was awaiting me."

Lucius stares at him with pure hatred. "You shut your fucking mouth! You help a slave bed my best gladiator and then steal from me, after I welcome you into my house! You drink my wine, eat my food, and then spat in my fucking face! Well, my *friend*," he began, sarcastically enunciating the word friend, "I know how you love a good gamble. So you *will be* betting your life, because you will be fighting in the arena. You can bet the Gods on that." Lucius storms out of the cell, screaming for the guards. "Shut the fucking door on this traitor!" Walking out to the ludus, he stares up to the stars then hears his wife still having a fit. He is still unclear on what the reason was for her temper—the missing mask, or Felicia laying with Radix. Lucius finally tires of hearing Camilla having her melt down and walks into her chamber. "Will you ever be finished with your fit of madness? I mean, I do not see why you are in such a raging fit? We will get our payback. Fuscus will be in the tournaments and I have spoken to Radix to give him notice that if he wins the next two fights he will be a free man. If he loses, he will be in my ludus and fighting for me until he dies!"

Camilla covers her mouth in shock.

Lucius turns around with a sneer. "Also, you go on and on about others, disgracing my name and my house. But you are the one that has no reason at all to speak ill of others, because it is you who has disgraced my name the most! Do you think I would not find out?"

Camilla takes a large drink of her wine then looks over at her husband. "What are you talking about, Lucius? I have done no such thing!"

Lucius spins around. "You fucking Radix! That is what I am speaking of. You would not have been so furious about Felicia and him lying together had you not had feelings of love for him! So, I decided that his winning will make him a free man and if by chance he loses—which I doubt he will—he will then stay in my ludus and you will be the one to leave, and I believe you going to the same island as Anton's wife, Lila, will do the trick. You can keep each other company. And if you both get so hot wanting affection from a man that you will not be seeing any cock, you can eat each other's cunts! You disgrace and humiliate me, woman, and the mere sight of you turns my stomach! So that sounds like wonderful payback. For your sake, you better hope that Radix wins! "

Camilla looks at him like she has had the wind knocked out of her. "What do you mean when you say I love Radix? He is a gladiator. How fucking ridiculous!" she yells, grabbing at her chest. Lucius looks at his wife, who is in utter shock of the outcome of the conversation. He storms out of the room, leaving her something to think about.

***

Cato stays to himself. He is still in shock and getting more infuriated as he finds out what the outcome has been on everyone. As he thinks of a punishment fitting for Calli and

Felicia, he almost breaks into tears until he hears Lucius walk up, talking to himself. Turning to his friend, he says, "Apologies, Cato, I must vent and I do not wish to take it out on one of my slaves because, truth be told, I would wind up fucking her to death because I am so mad. Cato, I am at a loss for words. I am still surprised that your slaves went and did this disrespectful thing behind your back. How disgraceful. But in two days Fuscus will be in the arena fighting for his life. Everything is happening too fast and I myself cannot believe it! My wife has gone mad, the man I once thought was my friend is a traitor, and my guards, along with the ludus teacher, are fucking fools!"

Cato then asks, "Oh; no worries, my friend. Everything has happened too fast for me as well. And the outcome is just still so shocking. It is hard to fathom and believe Fuscus could do this. He has been in my home many times and nothing has come up missing. But I do not have that many valuable possessions about my house. Did you say that in two days Fuscus will be in the arena to fight?"

"Yes, that is correct. Why?"

Cato shakes his head. "I see. With the outcome of everything that has just come to light, will there still be a feast tonight? I am hoping that the house will be in order for the guests when they arrive, and I will make sure that Calli and Felicia will help to do just that."

Lucius replies with a smile. "Yes! Fuck; yes, we will not let good food and wine go to waste! I believe there are enough slaves here that this place will be in order before they all arrive."

"Ok then. And please excuse me while I tend to my slaves," Cato says, making his way back in the villa. He overhears Calli and Felicia talking amongst themselves as he stands behind them and hovers. They are still kneeling and glaring at the floor. Cato shouts at them. "I did not say you could talk! Stand, both of you!" Calli and Felicia are startled at their Master's sudden burst of anger, standing as ordered, but still looking down. He then walks around in front of them and shouts. "Look at me." When they do, he continues to bark orders. "Disrobe- Now! Since you wish to humiliate me, I will do the same to the both of you. You will both wash the feet of the guests, and you will both still be serving tonight at the feast. You will both be serving the guests in the nude as human platters. And after the feast, you will sleep in the slave quarters tonight. I have been very good to both of you and more than fair than any other Master would be. And for you both to lie and treat your Master like this—just remember this: neither of

225

you will bring disrespect to me or my house again. Is that understood? If something like this ever happens again you will receive a punishment much worse," Cato says in a very stern tone.

Calli and Felicia look into Cato's eyes, answering in a firm, "Yes, Master."

They both reach up and begin untying their dresses, letting them glide off their bodies and onto the floor. Cato walks around both of the women. He can see the shame that they have done to him in their eyes and ignores the sadness and humiliation that he can feel coming from both women. He walks back, retrieving a glass of wine and noticing the other slaves hurry about to decorate the entire villa, readying the meats and fruit and then bringing up the many containers of wine.

"Go see what you can do to help get this feast ready," Cato says.

The two slaves walk into the feasting area where they begin setting up the food trays on the different tables.

***

Before the feast commences, Camilla makes her way to the slave quarters, trying to be as quiet as she can hoping that Lucius does not find out.

She walks into the room where Radix is sitting, noticing his saddened look across his face but paying no mind. "Do you love this slave bitch named Felicia?" Before he can answer, she continues to speak. "How dare you?! How could you even think that she was me?! Have you not felt my legs wrap around you enough times you would recall whose thighs tightened across your waist? Did her cunt feel like mine? With my breath on your skin enough times and my voice whispering your name and begging for more of your cock, I would think you would not forget that! I am still in total shock that you would even think she was me!"

Radix looks over at her says, "I did not know until that night that she would even remember me, Domina. But I cannot speak with false tongue any longer. Yes, I do love her!"

Camilla shudders in shock, throwing her head back and laughing hysterically. "You would rather love a slave than love me? You're Domina?" She feels so grotesque and disrespected that she was being over looked by her favorite gladiator and a slave had stolen his heart. She throws her glass of wine on Radix before stomping out. "Just so you know," she says before leaving, "Dominus knows about our affairs and he is livid. He says for your sake you better hope that you win. Because if you lose, you will go to the mines!" She stomps out, slamming the door behind her.

***

Felicia has just walked to the wine cellar. Getting to the last step, she loses her balance which causes her to trip and fall to the ground and scrapes her arms and leg. When she tries to get up, Camilla comes out from the locked gate and beings kicking Felicia in the stomach, grabbing her by the back of her hair, slapping her across her face. Then, she leans down and whispers in a cruel, evil tone, "You ruined him, you filthy whore. If you know what's best for you, you better stay out of my way tonight!"

Felicia picks herself up from the dirt floor after Camilla stomps up the stairs. Walking over to pick up the vase of wine and carrying it up the stairs, she tries her hardest not to wince from the pain Camilla has caused.

Calli, Felicia, and a few other slaves await the arrival of the guests. When the guests arrive, Felicia removes the guests' sandals while Calli washes and dries their feet. After everyone has arrived, the two go and wash their bodies off quickly then lay across a large marble, oval table. The other slaves cover their waists and upper legs with a cloth as another slave gently places fruit and pastries over Calli and Felicia's bodies then places a bowl of honey in each of the ladies hands and other sweetened dips next to each other. Their arms itch and are uncomfortable after only a few minutes, and their backs begin to tighten up as well the calves of their legs; shooting pains down to their ankles and Charlie horses across their feet. To say the least, the pain was agonizing and horrible. The women grit their teeth to try to ignore it.

The guests and slaves do not say a word to Calli and Felicia. The guests just walk around them picking food off of their bodies and placing it onto their napkins, while the slaves just add more desserts. Camilla and her lady friends enter into the room, laughing about that day's gossip. They stop and stare at Calli and Felicia lying on the table, giving each slave a dirty look.

Camilla looks down at Felicia, giving her a sneer look as says in a snobby tone, "Oh, this is the little nasty whore that ruined my Radix."

Hearing the other women gasp and cowl, Camilla picks up the honey and pours some over Felicia's face, smearing it across. "Clean my hands," she says.

Felicia closes her eyes tightly and scrunches her nose, trying to keep the sticky substance away.

***

Cato does not see Calli or Felicia until the feast is over and everyone has left.

He walks in the room, looking at both of them and noticing the crumbs and sauce all over their bodies. "Get up, wipe yourselves off, and go to bed," he commands. "We have to get ready for the games the day after." They both sit up, swinging their legs over and hopping off the table.

They clean their bodies off from all the crumbs and sticky substances and say, "Good night, Master Cato."

Cato doesn't say a word to neither of them. They slowly walk back to the slave quarters. Calli and Felicia weep heavily that night, not able to sleep at all.

Cato tries as hard as he can to sleep, but it will just not come to him. Just as the sun begins to rise, he walks around the villa to look at the different décor and the amazing flowers that are bigger than his head. They are a deep, dark, red color with thin yellow stripes around the petals. Another color is light purple with little pink specks and light green inside the petals.

They smell like a combination of honey suckles and roses. He finds himself standing out on the balcony as he sees a light rainbow form across the sky. The birds are awake and chirping. He looks down and notices a slave carrying a large container of wine. He can tell she is a very small frame woman, who is walking with a small limp. She was a pretty slave with curly brown hair. Her dark brown eyes are gorgeous, along with her pouty, red lips and perfect teeth. Cato wonders what her story was and why she is a slave here. He lets out a loud sigh and walks to the stairs to ask the slave if she is in need of assistance with the wine.

The slave looks at him in shock and nervously says, "No, Sir Cato. I have it. But thank you." She smiles, walking past him.

Cato wonders how his friend, Fuscus, is handling the lock up area, and how Calli and Felicia handled having to sleep in the slave quarters. He walks into the villa to question of the ladies' whereabouts, overhearing a few slaves speak of the actions of the night before. When the slaves see Cato and how quickly he was to anger that very moment, they quickly apologize then go silent, looking to the floor and rushing off to another part of the villa.

He sees Camilla and stops her. "I wish to see my slaves, Camilla, I did not see any guards, and I want to hurry to get to the amphitheater before it gets too busy."

Camilla nods her head, ordering a guard to go get them. She then walks off, trying to find Lucius, who was in the ludus giving his speech to the gladiators.

Chapter 10

Calli and Felicia sit on a small bench with their backs against each other. The slave area is so muggy and smelled horrible, like mold and rotten food. The other slaves in there were exhausted and miserable. The guard comes to the door, unlocking it and letting the slaves out for the day. Calli and Felicia go upstairs where they see Cato standing at the balcony. They can see he is still upset with the both of them and the sadness in his eyes breaks their hearts. They walk up with their heads bowed in shame from the night before.

They both walk up to their Master, kneeling at Cato's feet and weeping. "Master, many apologies on disgracing your name. We will never do that again. We never meant for this to happen. Will you ever be able to forgive us?"

Cato lets out a big breath, seeing these two women with such grace and how apologetic they are. "Your stupidities and actions have brought shame on my name. I do not know if I can trust you after the stunt you pulled last night. I can forgive you, but I do not know when, or if, I can forget." Calli and Felicia nod their heads.

***

"We shall speak of this later," Cato whispers. "Until then, you both go put on your dresses and get ready for the games."

Camilla and Lucius walk into the hall where Calli and Felicia are standing with the stream of tears still trickling down their face. Cato looks at Lucius, shaking his head as they hear thunder crash just outside the window and the winds begin to pick up, blowing rain inside the villa.

Lucius glances over and clears his throat. "Cato, I am sure everything will work out. This is a difficult day, and the gods even agree. Do you hear the rain fall from the skies?" he asks.

Cato wonders how Lucius can be in such a great mood when one of their dearest friends would soon be fighting for his life in front of all to see. Cato heard rumors of Fuscus being in agonizing pain from all the rain and pressure of the holding cells. It is no wonder people would go insane.

Cato asks loudly, "I hear that Fuscus is in horrid pain with his ears and he feels like he is going deaf. Is this true?"

***

234

Lucius looks over at Cato. "I heard that by the time a medic could get to him they had to put pressure inside one of his ears because the moisture and pressure from being underneath had caused his ear to get infected very badly! So yes, he was in plenty of pain."

"Do you mind if I go speak to Fuscus before the start of the games?"

"I have no problem with this. I, too, must ready for the games. The rain is falling again," he mused. "This will be an interesting and intriguing match. I suggest you go now before you run out of time."

***

The rain slows to a small trickle when Cato makes his way to Fuscus' cell and sees his friend, who, though he had only been in the holding area a few days, looked like he had been there for an eternity.

His friend was badly beaten by the guards. Fuscus' dark hair is matted together with the gray strands being ripped out. His face is not any better; he has deep wounds over his arms where a hot iron had been pressed into his skin, and his fingers were almost disfigured as well, being covered in blood and bruises. He still has two blackened eyes; one eye almost

235

swollen shut, and a dingy orange bruise across the bridge of his nose and a deep cut across his chin. His ability to walk was all off balance due to his ear drum being busted from the infection that had set in.

Cato stares at his friend, who only has a few hours before he is to fight. The cell is bone cold with pieces of straw and grass across the floor and a nasty bucket of muddy like water with a small ladle that was caked in dry mud to drink from. Cato feels so bad for his friend. The torture and humility he has been subjected to and what he was being accused of was not worth all of this. Cato asked Fuscus, "Why was the mask and goblet in your bag? It does not make sense."

Fuscus wipes his dirty hands covered in dried blood across his clothes and stares out the small window to the rain coming down even harder and the water splashes into the room, making a small puddle under his feet. "Cato, I have not a clue how those got in my possession. I had drank and celebrated with you and the others and stumbled back to my bed. When I arrived, there was a pretty slave and she told me that she was told to service me."

Cato looks at his friend and asks, "Did she say what her name was?"

Fuscus flops down on the bench that is stained with blood and other unknown substances, paying no mind to the rat that is running behind him when he says, "I would do anything to turn back time and hold my wife in my arms once more or have my son wrap his small hands around my fingers. It doesn't matter now; I will be meeting them shortly."

Cato stands by the window, watching the rain pour into the cell and trying to calm is friend. "You mustn't think that way, Fuscus! You are not weak; you are very strong! Just like a horse!"

"I am not sure about that." He sighed. I cannot recall the slave's name, but she did have red hair. The night I had with her was, simply put, amazing! How was I to know the following morning I would be treated worse than a dog and thrown into a cage?"

***

Calli and Felicia are in the guest quarters, dressing and fixing each other's hair. They walk down an empty corridor toward the front door where they wait patiently. They could not help but hear three slaves talking amongst themselves. The slave that was doing the majority of the talking was the one they had first met when they very first came to Lucius' home.

237

The slave stops next to Felicia and said, "Domina is very pissed at you and Radix for lying together. She has spoken to Dominus and he plans on selling Radix after the games tomorrow at the auction. Just think, it will be your fault, Scortum!" Calli's eyes widen and her mouth falls open. She bites her lip, not saying anything. The slave swings her hips as she walks pass Felicia. Felicia quickly grabs the slave girl's ankle as the slave falls to the floor. Felicia could not help herself as she burst into laughter. Calli bows her head and elbows her sister in the side as Felicia screams out, "Ouch! Calli, what was that for?"

The other two slaves are helping their friend up and giving Calli and Felicia an evil look.

***

Camilla hears the ruckus as she comes in and investigates as well. Camilla is outraged as she sees her slave being picked up from the floor, noticing the scrapes on the girls' arms and knees. "What did you do to my slave? If she is injured, I will make sure you will take her place until she is healed, and I know your Master will approve of this!"

Cato is in the arena of the ludus. He had just finished speaking with Fuscus when he hears the commotion. Entering the villa, he loudly says, "What in the name of Hades is going on in here? Why did you trip her? Which one of you tripped her? I tell you ... You are not making things easier on yourselves! And, yes, Camilla is correct; if her slave is too injured for her to do her chores and other jobs then you will stay here and serve under her until she is healed."

Calli shakes her head as she looks up at her Master. "I elbowed Felicia, Master. She was being... ornery. I had to do something."

Camilla leaves the room to check on her slave and returns to her chambers as Lucius walks in, interrupting everyone.

***

Lucius is in a great mood as he hums a song, walking up to Cato as he says in a cheerful tone, "Hello friend. It is last day of the games, and I do hope you have great luck on the betting portion. But poor Fuscus—at twilight he will be seeing his wife and child again."

Cato looks at Lucius and says, "Apologies, but a moment in private please?"

Lucius summons the two slaves to another room where another group of slave girls giggle as they watch the gladiators make their way upstairs. Cato and Lucius stand on the balcony as Cato says, "I spoke to Fuscus and he mentioned to me a slave being summoned to his room the night the masks went missing. He said that this slave has red hair, but could not recall her name. Would you happen to know of which slave he is speaking of? I do not recall a red headed slave at the feast."

Lucius nods his head. "Yes, I know Camilla gets a few new slaves a few times a year. She is normally in the kitchen area, but we figured with Fuscus not being with a woman in a very long time he would enjoy her. Her name is… Oh Fucks Sake! I cannot recall, but I am sure it will come to me," he says to Cato with a smile. "Let's head to the games. The women can follow with the guards."

Cato agrees before leaving, informing Calli and Felicia that they will follow with Camilla and her slaves as he walks out the door.

***

Since it is the last day of the games, Lucius insist that Cato and his slaves sit with them. The few slaves, Calli, Felicia, and Camilla walk past the vendors as a few men walk

240

out and show the ladies the small statues and wooden carvings, but they knew not to sell the knives. Camilla stops at a vendor, noticing the large statue and a very pretty tapestry hanging on the wall. It was of Hercules, and it was an eye catcher with all the vibrant colors.

The vendor picks up a small statue that matches the tapestry and says, "The Domina has more beauty than any Goddess. The Gods shall be jealous! Please, ma'am, take this small statue as a gift." Camilla is not that cruel or greedy; she did plan on paying the vendor.

Calli and Felicia stand in the back, not saying a word when they notice a red headed slave push between them. The other slaves standing next to Calli and Felicia whisper to them, "That is Jade. She works in the kitchen and delivers the gladiators their food. She is a snollygoster and a trepan!" Calli glances at the lady when she notices a small silver charm that is pinned to the inside of her dress. It is the same one that Fuscus had shown her. He kept it close to his heart in remembrance of his son who died.

All the women go to the amphitheater. The games have just started as Camilla and the slaves enter the area. The slaves stand and watch the gladiators stand side by side as they are introduced to the crowd. People look at their small tickets as

Lucius calls out the names of the fighters; his smile deepening as the crowd cheers. When the guards brought out Christians to the middle of the ring, they are chained together. The crowd laughs, throwing rotten food at them as they walk quickly. Camilla and Lucius laugh as they fill their glasses and eat off the silver trays filled with fresh fruits.

Lucius shouts out. "Blasphemy!"

Across the arena you could hear a woman scream. "The shits of the abyss they crawled out of kill them!"

There are no survivors from this match. It is so humid and hot that day and people are beginning to feel sick. Felicia notices two of Camilla's slaves talking amongst themselves and she overhears their conversation.

"I can't believe Jade was able to get that! That charm is pretty. I wonder how much it is worth and who gave it to her?"

"I wonder the same, but you do know that before coming here she was sold for being a thief from her last Master! Anyone else would be crucified, but you know how Domina is always giving people another chance."

"I know! I overheard Jade telling a guard she was in the one room that Fuscus is accused of stealing the masks from, but Fuscus is still set to fight in the last match. He goes up against Radix. And tomorrow Dominus plans on selling Radix! It is so sad."

"Sir Cato is a very nice man, but it would not surprise me if he sells one of his two slaves as well."

The two fall silent as the final match is about to begin. The guards march out with the armor and weapons. Radix enters on one side as Fuscus is dragged out from the other. Fuscus' bruised face and swollen eye are obvious signs of his pain. He walks unsteady on his feet, probably dizzy from the wounds. He tries hiding his fear, reaching for his sword then raising his hand to wait for the beginning of the fight. Camilla stands, applauding as Radix is helped into his armor.

***

Calli stands by Cato, tracing her hand down his arm. Cato sees her trembling so he folds his hand over hers and looks at her to give her a reassuring smile. She feels her face blush as she is returning the gesture. Felicia walks over to refill the glasses of wine. She cannot stand to watch as her friend is killed. Fuscus picks up the rusted sword with both hands. He turns to where Lucius is sitting. Lucius then raises his hand and begins the match.

Radix gives Fuscus an evil look and says, "Prepare to die by my sword, little man! You steal my Master's stuff and make me look like a fool! Once I kill you, I will be a free man!"

The crowd laughs as Fuscus runs circles, trying to get as far away from Radix as he can. "Radix, I did no such thing! Your Master and myself have been friends for some time."

Felicia returns to Cato's feet, leaning over the side to watch the crowd cheering loudly and noticing a woman open her dress to catch the fighters' attention. She shakes her bare breast at them. The people that are sitting around her laugh and point at how she is acting. Her husband grabs her arm, pulling her drunken self back to her seat. She leans over, giving her husband a rough kiss and then raising her glass of wine to the sky.

***

Jade rolls her eyes at the outcome as everyone around her cheers. She stands by the table as she prepares a small platter for Lucius, when another slave walks up to her. "Apologies, Jade, but after the celebration why did I see you exiting Domina's room the other night with a small piece of fabric wadded up?"

Jade looks at the girl with pure hatred as if she wanted to kill her and says under her breath, "If you know what is best for you, you will hold your tongue, you little bitch!"

All of a sudden, the crowd cheers as Radix runs at full speed toward Fuscus. Fuscus quickly raises his sword, blocking Radix then swinging it as if he was going to chop down a tree catching Radix in his bicep. Fuscus, without thinking, pushes Radix to the ground with his heavy boot then smashes the handle of his sword into his face. Radix is hurt as the blood falls out of his mouth, but takes his shield and smashes it into Fuscus' knee. He laughs when he hears something crunch then gets to his feet.

***

Felicia overhears bits of the conversation of the two slaves in between the roaring cheers of the crowd. Felicia traces her fingers down her Master's leg looking up at him. Cato glances down, giving her a small smile. She feels a bad feeling deep down in her gut when the crowd's cheers fall silent.

"Well, it doesn't matter anyway. Besides, in a few minutes Fuscus will be dead and tomorrow Radix will be sold!" Felicia jumps up when she hears Jade speak these

245

words. She is finally putting the missing pieces together! Felicia hurriedly goes to Cato's side and kneels down, "Master! You must listen to me; please!"

Cato leans in and says, "This better not be another way to disrespect my name or so help me, I will take my whip to you! I have not done this in a very long time, but I will do just that!"

Felicia shouts, "NO! It's not going to bring disrespect to your name or your house! I swear to the gods above."

Cato shakes his head, leaning in to hear what she has to say. Cato turns to her in shock as he stands up quickly, knocking over his food and drink. Lucius and Camilla glare at him as if he has gone mental. "Cato! What is the matter?"

Cato looks at Lucius before shouting out. "STOP THE FIGHT! My friend, please listen to me. It is of the upmost importance that you put a stop to this fight!"

Lucius then looks down at the two men and screams as loud as he can. "HAULT, STOP!" Radix and Fuscus stand frozen, looking up at Lucius in puzzlement. Lucius springs to his feet and asks, "What in the name of Apollo is wrong with you, Cato?"

"Yes, what is it, Cato?" Camilla questions.

"Fuscus is innocent! Your slave, Jade, set him up!"

The arena goes silent. Lucius has no other choice but to stop the match. They all make their way to the villa. Jade is escorted by guards to an empty cell under the ludus. All kinds of commotion is going on; Fuscus and Radix are sent into the physician for their injuries whose room is under the ludus. Lucius, Camilla, Cato, Calli, and Felicia are in the front room as they speak to the two slaves and hear the story. Lucius is furious at what has been brought to light. He goes through his papers, trying to find out prior reasons why Jade was sold. "AH HA! I found it! Let us see. Oh, Cato, you have to see this!"

-Jade- slave-sold- reason* Accused of stealing her Dominus gold coins* price paid for purchase 15 ASE

-Jade- slave- sold -*reason- Selling a necklace that belonged to her Domina and blaming another slave* price paid for purchase 15 ASE

-Jadeah- slave- sold- reason* Trying to stab another slave.* Price paid for at purchase 16 ASE.

Cato glances at the paper in disbelief as Camilla yells, "Bring Jade to us!"

247

The guards return with Jade. Her wrists are tied together and her reddish hair is covering her face as she gives Cato a dirty look. Camilla, filled with a fit of madness and humiliation, walks over to Jade and slaps her across her face as hard as she can, the sound echoing through the villa. "What the fuck is wrong with you? Are you a crazed person?" Jade looks up, smiling. Camilla sees this and raises her hand to slap her once again until Cato grabs her wrist. Everyone is quiet as Camilla stands with pure hatred and glares at Jade like a wild animal ready to attack. "You disrespect my home, my name, and our friends… you will receive thirty lashes!"

Cato stares at Jade and then says, "Jade, why on earth would you do this? You're Dominus and Domina have done so much for you; you would betray them like this?"

Jade then stares at the floor, not answering. Lucius screams, "You little lying, traitorous, back stabbing cunt! You answer him now!"

She finally answers, looking up at him. "I thought it was your slave, Calli's bag I put the stuff in. I was going to murder Fuscus and cut and injure myself, placing the blame on you! But in the morning when I awoke, Fuscus was already gone to market." The room fell silent as they looked at each other.

248

"Why; what did Cato ever do to you?"

Jade smarted off, "How would you feel being used as a betting tool for a game of dice? Then being told you are no longer their slave but to another man?! "When I saw Cato the first time he visited here, I was setting the trays for the feast. I noticed he had not one slave but two! I was heartbroken and jealous." She wept.

***

A while later, Radix and Fuscus are brought into the room. Calli and Felicia are kneeling on each side of Cato. Lucius hugs Fuscus, apologizing and then looking down at Jade. "I have no pity for you! As my wife ordered, thirty lashes will be your punishment. However, I order that she is to be sold immediately to the mines. It will not wait until morning." The guards bow their heads as they agree to do so and remove Jade.

Lucius and Camilla stand in front of Radix with a large smile over their faces. "Gladiator Radix," Lucius begins, "you have brought my house many blessings with coin that the gods rained down on us. And many splendid things, as well."

"Thank you Dominus, Domina. I am proud to have served your house."

249

Lucius nods and continues. "I had to make a choice; selling you or giving you your freedom. This is a hard decision; I did lose sleep many nights deciding on what to do. I have asked the goddess of wisdom to guide me in the correct path." Radix begins to sweat and has a nervous look on his face. Lucius lets out a loud sigh as he says, "Radix... I offer you your freedom, but also something else in return."

Radix stands in shock. "Thank you Dominus! Domina!"

Lucius continues. "You are very welcome, but I want to offer you a position in the Roman Army. I do hope you accept my offer."

Cato clears his throat. "Wonderful news, indeed. I have news of my own, if I may?"

Radix interrupts Cato and says, "Cato, if I may say: I wish to put my earnings toward Felicia's debt. With your approval, I wish to marry her one day." Calli grabs Felicia's hand, squeezing it tightly as she holds her breath.

Cato chuckles and scratches his head. "Radix that is impossible. That is hard to do; I did not place coin on her. I was about to say—" As Cato glances over to Felicia and notices her eyes filling up with tears, he gestures to her. "Please stand, Felicia." Felicia is so nervous, she stumbles to her feet as she holds onto Cato's arm and stands beside the man she loves, swaying back and forth. It all feels like a dream. "I too grant Felicia her freedom." The crowd gasped, but stayed silent otherwise. "But, since I did not place coin on her, and though I am very happy for the two of you, I cannot be the one to approve of this engagement. Anton will have to be the one to approve of this."

***

Anton enters the room in shock, having seen the entirety unfold. He walks up to Felicia and gives her a hug before he speaks. "Sweet Felicia, I have thought of you as a daughter to me for a very long time. Is what you really wish for?" he asks.

Felicia feels faint as she responds with a nod and then finds her voice. "Oh yes, Sir Anton! This is what I wish for!" Anton looks over to Cato, nodding his head in approval. "Well then, I say as of this day forward Radix and Felicia are engaged to be married! Felicia, I believe you have a locket in your possession?"

Felicia looks at Anton in surprise. "Yes, I do, but how do you know of that item?"

He smiles and says, "When Camilla and I purchased you, it was in your items from auction. I know it was your locket from your parents, so I knew to hold on to it. I did have it cleaned and put a new white ribbon in place of the brown basket weave that was going through it before. I do hope that is ok?"

Felicia shifts from one foot to the other and then jumps into Anton's arms, giving him a big hug. "Yes! Oh my goodness, yes! I am so thankful and very surprised that you did this. I appreciate that nice gesture. You are like a father figure to me." Everyone stands in silence as they see Cato raise his hands and gently remove her collar.

***

Calli cannot take the excitement anymore and jumps to her feet to hug her friend. Calli is so happy for Felicia and Radix. Camilla and Lucius smile brightly as they, too, are in shock from hearing the news. Felicia shrieks with excitement as she hugs Radix. Lucius smiles and is happy for him, calling for wine.

He then sits down and says, "I cannot believe I am saying this, but your winnings for today. I will give you ¾ of that I received for your match. This should be a great start to a new beginning of your new life as a freed man."

***

Radix accepts the position in the Roman Army and everyone prepares for the wedding. Radix ties a thick dandelion stem around Felicia's left ring finger then slowly slips it off and hands it to Fuscus for his future bride's ring. Since Felicia does not have a life locket or never knew her father, the closest one to a father figure she has is Anton.

The engaged couple are seen numerous times holding hands around the town within next few weeks. Anton is so happy for Felicia. He gives her a wedding dress that he has found. It is a full, one piece; the color a plain white wool, and it just reaches her feet.

Felicia is so nervous and excited that she almost forgets that she has to find flowers to place in her headpiece. With Lucius' permission, she walks in the small field outside the ludus and around the medium size garden area. With the help of Calli, they both begin making Felicia's headpiece, while Fuscus and his assistant quickly make a wedding ring out of pieces of a sword that belonged to Radix.

Fuscus takes the small stem that was tied around Felicia's finger and begins heating the thin cut metal, hammering small holes in the top for the small jewels to be placed. The ring is heated until it is bright red, almost the same as lava, and then quickly places it in water, allowing it to cool. It is then placed on top of the stem, making sure it is the exact size. Fuscus then has his helper use the small vice grips and gently remove her small reddish orange jewels that are the shape of a diamond taken out of her collar, and gently presses them in place around the ring.

The night before the wedding, Felicia stands in an empty room with only her and Calli. She stares at herself in the mirror that hangs on the wall, the headpiece over her head. The flowers she had picked earlier that day were a pretty shade of purple with pink spots, and white dandelions that are woven through the veil. The veil is connected to the base of the headpiece and it falls perfectly around the crown of her head and just down to her chin.

Felicia looks at her best friend. "I cannot believe tomorrow I will be the wife of Radix! I am so nervous, Calli!"

Calli looks at her friend as small tears begin to trickle down her cheeks. "I am so happy for you, Felicia! And I am so thrilled you have found your soul mate!"

Calli wraps a belt around Felicia's waist, tying it into a knot known as the "The knot of Hercules." Now only her husband can untie it. The day of the wedding, one of the priests stands in the entry way of Lucius and Camilla's villa. They both give the consent to use their home for the ceremony rather than making the travel to Anton's villa. Those in attendance of this happy occasion were Lucius and Camilla, Anton and his lady friend, Cato and Calli, Fuscus and his slave, plus one more couple. There are ten total witnessing this. Radix and Felicia stand in front of the priest while holding hands. She is so happy as she turns to her soon to be husband and saying in front of those present, "Quando tu Gaius, ego Gaia"—When and where you are Gaius, I then and there am Gaia. Then the priest makes an offering to Jupiter of the ceremonial cake, and then the bride and groom ate from the same cake to officiate the marriage. After the celebration, the newlyweds make their way to their new home.

***

Calli has mixed feelings; she's happy for Felicia, but at the same time she is sad from feeling like she is losing her best friend. Calli runs up to Felicia and gives her a huge hug, whispering in Felicia's ear, "I am so happy for you, and you are more than my friend! You are my sister!"

Chapter 11

Cato can tell how much this hurts Calli and, honestly, deep inside a small piece of his heart is breaking from not being able to follow in the footsteps of his friends. He does his best at hiding his tears, walking up to Felicia and kissing her on the cheek.

"I will have your possessions delivered to your new home."

He, Calli, Fuscus depart on their journey home, only stopping to rest and eat a meal. Calli is still so upset that she only picks at her food while Fuscus and Cato talk amongst themselves; Fuscus still in surprise of everything that had taken place so quickly.

"I do not know how to thank you, Cato! You saved my life. And I had no clue Jade was once your slave!"

Cato looks at his friend and says, "Yes, but I had honestly almost forgotten about Jade until you brought up that you were with a red head that night. I still remember how mean and perverse I used to be until I had her. She was the hardest headed, unruly slave I've ever had!" They both laugh, finishing their drinks before returning on their journey.

Calli cannot help but hear what the two men are conversing about. It does hurt her feelings and she cannot help to feel a bit alone. Who will Calli speak to now? She is very quiet the rest of trip home and cannot wait until that time comes.

The moon has just come peeking out of the cloudy night sky. With the temperatures having dropped so quickly, the flowers have started to slowly die from the freezing chills of the wind blowing in from the mountains. When the wind hits her skin, it feels like needles going through all the parts of your body. Calli's hands are shaking and are so cold that they are red and numb; her lips quiver and her teeth chatter loudly. She has never been so thankful to finally see the door of the villa, and she runs in to warm herself and begin putting her and Cato's belongings away.

Fuscus and Cato stand just inside the corridor of the villa, discussing what they will be doing next. Fuscus stands closer to the brick wall that has a torch burning brightly, rubbing his hands together, his ear aching from it being injured and giving him agonizing headaches. He breathes out a big sigh of relief after a few moments. "I am not sure where I will be heading. I do recall your sister, Sarah, telling me I was more than welcome to stay with her and Eric for a bit and I just may take them up on that invite. After all, I believe I deserve a vacation…if I do say so myself."

Cato nods his heads, chuckling loudly. "True! That you do, my friend, and I will say is not only are you a great blacksmith but the gods have also blessed you with jewelry making. That ring that you made for Felicia would make Venus herself jealous!"

"Well, I will not be leaving for my journey just yet. I still have to shoe some horses and make sure my slave is taken care of. But I will keep you posted. I bet it will feel differently with only having Calli here." He paused and lowered his voice. "You can tell she is very sad. But you never answered was if you are falling in love with this slave. I wonder what the people would think of that. The great Cato loving a slave! Honestly, if it were me and I loved a woman I would not care who knew!" Fuscus exclaims.

Cato gives Fuscus a dirty look and says, "That is easier said than done. I cannot say that I do or do not love her, because I do not know if I do. She does make me happy. But I am thinking that she may be better off if I were to just release her. Though I spent all that coin on her and she has been worth it. I recall when I purchased Calli at that auction. I know the people there thought I was insane for purchasing her at such a high amount, and I know the ladies in the auction house thought she was crazed going on that she was a "Princess". But, I wonder at times. She never acted like a wild person and at times how she speaks—. So, answer me this… what princess knows how to build a fire, make and mend clothes, and knows how to cook? She could be better off and happier if I released her. She could even find a mate."

Fuscus looks at his friend and can tell he is so confused at what he is doing. "Well, I do not know, Cato, but you do what you feel is best. I am sure if you free Calli, she will understand. But, you can see how much she does truly care for you. So just take it easy on her. You are my friend, but Calli is my friend, too."

The men go their separate ways. As Fuscus leaves, Cato can tell that the cold winds have finally stopped for some time.

***

Cato stands by a fireplace, glancing around his villa, and notices how quiet it is without Felicia there. He grabs a glass of wine while looking through the window and notices the trees have already started to lose leaves and the limbs are hanging low to the ground from the weight of the ice and snow as the winter chill and wind blows through them. He looks over to the couch that is tattered and torn, and it reminds Cato of how hard it had been until Calli came into his life.

Calli did brighten his day and finally gave him a reason to exist. He always wondered how his life would be had she not came to him. He recalls the rainbow that appeared over the auction house the day Fuscus talked him into going back to the auction and his eyes as they connected to him. He then thought about his wife and how much he missed her. He did not know what to do. What would happen if he did love Calli? What would everyone think? Should he listen to Fuscus' advice and just not give two fucks?

***

Calli walks in the room, seeing Cato glaring out the window to the very violent snow storm that has quickly approached the area. She walks up to him and catches a faint scent of the cinnamon and pine that crackles and burns in the fireplace. Her mouth waters as she sees his bare skin as it glistens from the small beads of sweat that are rolling down him. Calli just wants to touch him. It has been so long since he last touched her; before Felicia was married. She wanted, no needed to feel his skin against hers. She could not recall the taste of his lips, or the feeling of them against hers. She bites her lip and swallows hard as she reaches up and slowly places her fingertips against his skin, barely tracing down his muscular back and watching as the muscles twitch ever so slightly. Cato snaps out of his memory and spins around to grab her wrist, gripping it tightly.

"Many apologies," Calli utters. "I was just checking on you, and you looked in deep thought Master," she says while hanging her head.

Cato shakes her slightly. "Never do that to a soldier! Remember, I use to be an Officer in the Roman Army! I used to be able to snap a man's neck, almost twisting it off his shoulders or smash his brains out with my shield! I could have—Fuck! I could have snapped your neck before you even knew what would have happened. I am fine! I have been fine before you came here to serve my house, and I will be fine long after you are gone!"

Calli looks at him in confusion. "After I am gone? If I may ask, Master, what do you mean by that?" She reaches out to try to hug him. He looks up to her hypnotizing eyes then her lips. He snaps back. "You need not worry! I do not want you to touch me! Kneel and leave me be!" he snaps, quickly turning away as a small growl leaves his mouth.

Calli quickly kneels down, her back straight, hands on her thighs, with her head up looking at her Master's back. She sees the snowflakes falling against the window as she weeps low, trying to understand his sudden outburst and watching his shadow falling against the wall. Cato looks out the window to the sky, the snow suddenly stopping. The sky begins to clear and the stars are shining.

"What have I done to have you speak to me in such a way, Master?" Calli quietly whispers. "Do I not make you proud? Do you miss Felicia? I have done nothing but be faithful and respectful to you."

Cato turns around after a brief moment. "Do you make me proud? Stand!" he shouts. Calli quickly stands to her feet and he begins to walk toward her as his eyes turn a yellowish color, like that of a wolf stalking its pray, from the reflection of the fire in the distance. Calli begins to walk backward, trying to watch her surroundings as she glances behind her to make sure to not trip over articles that are strung about the floor. Just as she turns her head back around, he catches her off guard.

Cato rushes to her, scooping her up and wrapping her legs around his waist and her hands around his neck. Then he presses her against the rather cold brick wall, kissing her with all the force he has inside of him and grinding his cock against her moistened cunt. She has her eyes closed tight, breaking the kiss and gasping for air. She runs her hand across his forehead as she quietly pants into his ear. Cato slowly nibbles her neck, yanking her head back and tracing her neckline with the tip of his tongue. This sudden action leaves her unable to collect her thoughts as she begins tearing at his pants, kissing him back with the same force.

Cato then takes his hands, placing them on both sides of Calli's face and then says, "Look at me." The sudden action takes Calli's breath away. She opens her eyes, staring into his grayish blue. She presses her wetness against him, moving her hips back and forth "Damn it, Calli, I want you so fucking bad! Like I have never wanted anybody in a very long time!" Taking his strong hands, he yanks and strips her of her dress. Calli lets out a whimper of delight, the feeling of his warm breath on her skin with him leaning down sucking her perky breast between his lips makes her shriek and grasp her nails in his shoulders. He presses her harder against the wall as she begins to moan from the feeling of his teeth that glide across her hardened nipple. She leans up, sliding her hand across her pussy that is dripping of wetness, then placing it over to Cato's swollen and enlarged cock; gripping it just enough and feeling it pulsate as she moves her hand up and down slowly. Cato growls low in her ear. "I can't believe I am saying this, but stop." Grabbing her harder, he digs his nails in her ass while pressing her into him and then spinning around quickly and placing her across the couch.

Calli feels like she is in a dream as she feels Cato between her legs, her knees together and ankles apart. He slides his hands gently up between her legs, slowly prying them apart. He positions himself with the hardness of his cock pressing against her pussy until she feels just the head of him teasing her as he traces it across her slit and leans down to place his hand over her breast, squeezing hard with his nails pinching her tender skin; kissing her deeply as she hears the fire crackling. She opens her legs wide to welcome him in.

He looks at Calli, pushing a few strands of hair away from her face as she gives him a warm smile. Cato then blurts out, "Calli, I love you!" The room is quiet, with no response from her. Immediately, he regrets his words. "Fuckin' shit! NO, NO NO…" Standing up, Cato pulls his pants back up "Apologies, but I must remove myself," he says as he walks out of the room.

Calli lies on the couch for a brief moment, thinking, *what in all of Rome just happened?* Master Cato told her he loved her! She quickly jumps up and still can't believe her ears. She cannot lie to him or herself any longer; she must tell him that at one point in time she was a princess. Throwing a dress on and quickly rushing out the door, she goes in search of him.

***

Cato stands next to the partially frozen waterfall, the crystallized particles twinkling off the beams of the moon that are shining down as he punches the half frozen water and grits his teeth as the skin is ripped from his knuckles from the frigid ice cutting deep into his flesh, blood beginning to run from his injuries.

He yells to the heavens, hoping for an epiphany from the Gods. "My name is supposed to mean 'wise', yet I have no clue of what to do! In all honesty, I do love Calli, but I cannot do this. It is wrong. If she is a princess, then I need to give her freedom. Apollo, I ask you to give me strength because I am so lost."

***

Calli sees Cato looking up to the sky just as she sneaks up to him just as he is finishing his prayer and turns around and glares at her through his blood shot eyes. He says, "What happened back there? I did not mean that to happen."

265

"What do you mean, that you did not mean this to happen?" Calli asks.

Cato wipes his eyes of the tears he had shed, releasing a big sigh. "Nothing. It has been a very long, tiresome few days away, Calli."

Calli looks at him and shouts, "Oh, do not give me that shit! Oh no, not now. You tell me you love me then you say that you didn't mean it. You, at times, can be just downright mean and very confusing!"

"Excuse me? You have forgotten I am still your Master. Do not ever speak to me in that tone again," Cato yells at her, shaking his head and then making his way back to the villa.

Calli follows him closely. She is right on his heels as they both walk in swiftly into Cato's study. "What are you searching for?" Cato tosses everything around the table as he begins rummaging through papers and throwing things to the floor in a fit of madness. His face lights up as he notices the small scroll that he found that was in a small vase on one of the book shelves. The scroll is wrapped tightly in a red ribbon. Clenching the scroll tightly, he then turns around and glares at

Calli. She stares at him, curious as to what he will do with the scroll that he holds tightly in his hand.

"What is that in your hand? Please tell me what is in your possession."

"I remember when I bought you. You told the ladies at the auction house that you were a princess. I need to know, is this true?"

Calli stops and stares, giving him a blank look.

"Is it true? Tell me now!"

Calli jumps at the sound of his voice and then yells back at him. "Yes! This is true; I was once a princess. So what? I do not see what the big deal is! Have you just not paid attention and realized that I have never tried to run away?! From that very moment when you purchased me at the auction house, I have been yours. I belong to you! I do not even know who that person was back then! But I do know who I am now."

Cato lifts his head as he takes in a deep breath. "I am sorry, but, I cannot do this. I can no longer keep you as my own, and I cannot call you mine. You have a family elsewhere that you need to find. I will be better off alone." He quickly flicks his wrist and the scroll unrolls and hits the floor, revealing Calli's papers from the auction. He holds the scroll up and whispers. "You are now free." He drops the paper to the candle and lights it aflame.

Calli has no clue what to do first; whether to save her owner papers or run after Cato after he walks out of the room.

Calli runs after Cato, finally catching up to him. "Master, please tell me what I can do to please you and I will do that!"

Cato turns to her with his mouth open and says, "Damn it, I said you are free! You have no reason to call me Master, Calli. It's just more… it's now gotten an all new kind of complicated."

Cato turns around and screams. "Go away, Calli, or Helena—whatever your name is! Just leave! I grant you your freedom! I am better off alone. I am so fucking broken and fucked up. I cannot hurt anyone else. Especially you, *Your Highness.*"

Calli falls to her knees as she feels like her heart has been ripped from her body and stomped on. She feels the tears fall to the dampened, thawed grass. Calli stands up and follows Cato. She finds him standing on a hill and he looks like he is furious with the world. Calli slowly walks over to him and says, "Master, no, I do not understand. Why would you say that you love me and then ask me to leave? And what is so complicated that you cannot tell me?"

Cato turns to her, throwing his hands to the air and shaking his head as he goes to walk away once again, nudging her out of his way.

"You are a very hard-headed man, just like a donkey!" Calli yells back at him, grabbing his arm and trying to turn him toward her. "Cato, you know what? Fuck it! I can tell that you are a very strong man! You are not going to hurt me. I know this. What; do you not love me?"

"I am not that strong, Calli. Do not fool yourself. And yes, I do love you! Ok? See, that is what the problem is—I am in love with you and you are a slave… I mean, a princess. Ha! I am even confusing myself!"

Calli begins to cry as she says, "I love you, too! Cato, you are the one who helped heal me. When I was lost, you were the one who found me and put my broken pieces back together. That was you, Cato! It has always been you!" Cato finally realizes that he has to be with her and to keep her. He picks her off the ground and then grabs Calli by her shoulders and pulls her as closely as he can to him. He traces the tips of his fingers over her face and lifts her chin, wiping her tears away and follows it with a deep, passionate kiss. He stops briefly to look deep into her eyes. "No, my sweet Calli, you healed me. I thank the gods that allowed us to be able to find each other. I promise you this: nothing will ever separate us again. I love you; always have and always will!"

The skies begin to dance with different rays of colorful lights of blues, greens, and pinks. The stars then began to fall like rain drops from a cloud toward the earth. Calli looks at Cato and whispers, "I think your questions were heard."

He smiles, holding her close to him. They both stand together watching the stars as they dance across the skies following the bluish auroras that are side by side. Cato looks at Calli, watching her face light up as the lights shoot down from the heavens.

"Before you came to my place and before you were a slave, where was your home, Princess?"

Calli looks at him in surprise and says, "Well, I use to be from Scotiania."

"When was the last time you saw your family?"

"Oh, it has been many moons. My parents allowed me to travel with my fiancé, Justus. He was the one who sold me to the auction house."

Cato hugs Calli tightly. "I have never traveled there to your lands."

Calli smiles. "I would love to see my parents and my brothers and sisters once again."

She slides her hand across her golden collar with the pink pearls.

"What do I call you now? Calli or Helena?" Cato questions.

She gazes up to the sky with a warm smile across her face then gazes into his eyes and says, "I will no longer be known as Helena, and since coming here I am no longer a princess. But I will always be *your* Calli, and you are my Prince that rescued me once upon a time!"

Cato stands to his feet, pulling her to him as he gently kisses her lips and whispers in her ear. "So, tell me? When do we leave on our adventure, my sweet Calli?"

"Do you mean to Scotiania?" Calli questions with a big smile across her face.

271

Cato laughs and says, "Yes, my sweet, loving Calli, to Scotiania!"

Calli smiles. "Anytime; as long as I am with you!"

GLOSSARY

Ludus –a school for Gladiators.

Scortum- Low class whore.

Denari- Silver

Aurei- Gold (95%)

Aes- Bronze

25 Denari (silver) = 1 gold coin

ABOUT THE AUTHOR

Roxie McDugger is a mother of three very active sons and a proud Army spouse. She grew up in a small town in Illinois, just minutes from St. Louis, Missouri and now resides in the Anchorage, Alaska area. When she's not writing, she enjoys several other activities. She's a passionate woman and writer and hopes readers enjoy her work.

You may find her here:

https://www.facebook.com/RoxieMcDuggerAuthor

http://planettopiapublishing.com/

www.ingramcontent.com/pod-product-compliance
Lightning Source LLC
Chambersburg PA
CBHW070900180626
46817CB00003B/847